What's the Catch?

A Novel by

K. Newman

ISBN:150245081X
ISBN-13:9781502450814

1 . Fiction: online dating
2. Fiction: adult relationships

DEDICATION

FOR THE ISLANDERS

CONTENTS

ACKNOWLEDGMENTS

Thank you Carl Voyles for making this happen;

M. Clark, editing.; Alan Mitchell, punctuation police.

Plenty of Fish

After more than nine months of trying to decide whether Scott and I were really over, I knew that we at least ought to be, over. My sisters had encouraged and applauded my decision to leave him. My island friends, especially those who knew us both and knew that Scott had moved onto other women within the first month of our breakup, also urged me to get out there and find someone new.

There seemed to be no going back, even if the comfort of being with someone grew more attractive with each passing day. I felt lonely and desolate. I really did not know how to go about finding someone new; Scott and I had just stumbled upon each other while browsing in an art studio, began talking and were practically inseparable afterwards.

I would never consider frequenting the local bars, or attending discos or other places where singles might meet at night. There was an intense fear of meeting another alcoholic who, like my deceased husband, I wouldn't recognize as such until too late—recognizing a drinking problem after I had already become involved and thinking I could handle it. No. A man dependent on drink to make his day complete I did not want. I went to bed around 9 p.m. every evening and enjoyed getting up to watch the sunrise. I could keep busy throughout the day with pilates and pickleball at the gym, coffee with my islander friends, swimming, biking around the island, shopping, running with the dog, playing mah jongg with the ladies at the club, and tutoring at the local elementary school. I had learned how to fill my days so there was virtually no time left over, but it was during those hours from 5 p.m. to 9 p.m. that I became acutely aware of my loneliness.

Don, a man my age who lived in the neighborhood, often stopped by after dinner time with his dog. We would take walks with both charges tugging us along, often out for over an hour at a time, stopping at the Gulf to watch the sunset from the edge of the beach. Dogs were not allowed on the white sandy beaches of the island.

Don was good looking, fun, talkative and would bring over movies and books on CD that he thought I might enjoy. The drawback was that he was a lifelong bachelor who lived with his mother. It seemed unlikely to me that a man my age would ever marry if he hadn't already. When asked whether he ever wanted to marry, he had only replied, "I've had some propositions in my time." Apparently he had never asked a woman to marry him. I doubted that I would be the first.

He sometimes touched my arm in passing, but it went no further than that. Once we ran into neighbors who invited us to a party. He declined. He hadn't even consulted with me, even though I was standing at his side. It was not a good sign.

I saw Don as a nice companion, and good friend, but seemingly not boyfriend material, or to be taken seriously when it came to romance. He had just left town to head north for the summer. That left another void. The fun we had just taking walks together in the cooling evening hours was missed and left another reminder of the reality of the isolation of living alone. It was time for me to do something other than mope about feeling sorry for myself. My life was not over at 60 and I had to make something more of it.

Playing pickleball at the gym one morning, a 68-year-old woman mentioned she was dating. She said she used a website called Plenty of Fish to find dates. She was no beauty, but she stayed fit, and looked her age. She suffered from a physical impairment which left her with a mild limp.

If she could find a date, I thought, then so could I! I could still be found attractive by men, if there were any out there I could find.

There seemed to be virtually no eligible single men on the island. I knew this for a fact, since my islander coffee crowd was also keeping an eye out for me. It was time to expand horizons and look outside my friendly but small town, devoid of eligible single men of similar age.

Aha: Google might be the answer! I typed in "Dating". Hundreds of possibilities presented themselves. I chose to explore the "Top Ten Dating Websites" and was overwhelmed with the choices that were presented. There seemed to be a website for every type of situation and person. I took a quick look at many of them:

1. Zoosk: $29 monthly fee and poor reviews for having to pay for messaging;

2. Match.com: only free to look at profiles with registration;

3. eHarmony: Scott used this and paid semi-annual fees. It was annoying to think he purported to be looking for a long lasting, committed relationship;

4. OurTime: designed for singles over age 50 looking for dates;

5. Howaboutme: casual daters over age 25;

6. ChristianMingle: devoted to Christians;

7. Mate1.com: casual and serious lovers;

8. BlackPeopleMeet.com: specialized site;

9. JDate: exclusively for Jewish singles;

10. *POF:* "Plenty of Fish" purported to be used by over 80 million daters, reporting innovative compatibility testing.

Then there were a myriad of even more specialized services: ProfessionalSinglesOnline, just dating, sex encounters, meeting widowers, e-vow for those who were intent on marriage, even sites for specific ethnic backgrounds like Italians.

Hello! Why had I waited so long?

By eliminating sites that required fees for service, and specialized sites that didn't pertain to me, I narrowed down my choice to Plenty of Fish, aka *POF*.

The first step was to fill out a profile, a series of questions with answers provided in boxes.

It started with *The Basics*: describe your personality—I chose athletic, since I was trying to exercise two hours every day. It asked for what type of person one was seeking—I chose "Male," followed by *Intent,* for which I chose long-term. I certainly wasn't out for casual dating, or ready for marriage. The basics required a first name, city of residence, state, zip code and duration of longest relationship. It was easily competed in a few minutes.

POF then asked for *Personal Information*, which again was quite simple to complete: marital status, height, body type, hair color, religion, ethnicity, profession, income level.

It then asked if you smoked, if you would date someone who smoked, did drugs, drank (and if so how often), owned a car, had children, wanted more children, and whether you would date someone who had kids.

POF wanted to know education level. I hesitated with this since Juris Doctorate was not a choice, nor was doctorate. There also was not a choice for MD. I chose graduate degree as my level, even though JD was a form of doctorate. How many kids did my parents have? (Why would that be relevant?) The rest were easy—eye color, birth order, second language, do you have pets, whether you would date someone "BBW", followed by whether you were ambitious. I pondered the meaning of "BBW", then determined, since it was followed by a question asking if you would date someone with a few extra pounds, that my answer should be "no". I worked hard to maintain my weight and so should anyone I wanted to date.

Next came the hard part, the part I hadn't been ready to prepare. It asked for three things: *Headline*, a mandatory *Description*, and an optional description of a *First Date*.

The suggestion was that to be successful, one should talk about hobbies, goals, what makes you unique, as well as one's taste in music. For my *Headline*, I chose "Let's Talk," since I figured that was where anything would start. For *Description*, I chose to talk about myself and came up with what I thought was an accurate description of my typical day:

There's nothing I enjoy more than a bike ride around the island with my dog Trooper running alongside me. He's an 8-year-old retriever I inherited from my children. He loves to run and since he is usually too strong for me to walk for long, biking works well and keeps him exercised. We make it a habit to go out in the evenings to watch the sunset and catch the Gulf breezes. He stays tied under the shady Australian pines which border the beach while I take a dip in the clear, tepid waters.

I go to the gym every morning and play pickleball for an hour or two with a bunch of friendly and physically fit retirees. Usually it's easiest for me to exercise with other people, and the time goes by quickly when engaged in a game. I was averaging six days every week, but the hours will be cut with summer approaching and children using the Center. I am looking for an alternative, and cooler climates to visit during the summer months.

I've had fun in the past months helping a friend edit her children's book she's writing. I've joined a few clubs, and am involved in some parish activities since I moved to the island a few years ago after my husband died. Making new friends has been easy, but finding a good man to date has been a challenge!

I sat back and felt satisfied with my description. It would let whoever read it know I kept busy with simple but satisfying activities. I didn't want to appear too lonely or needy to take on a man in my life. Desperation never looked good, I thought, as I recalled one of Scott's last calls to me. He was crying and begging me to come back. It was sad, but I wasn't ready to return to a relationship in which I felt I was no longer his priority. He hadn't been willing to give me time to think things over before he moved on. When I had suggested we meet again, just a month afterwards, he was already seriously involved with another woman.

POF asked for a description of a *First Date*.

I suggested "coffee at a local café on the island, followed by a walk along the beach."

As for *interests*, I could list swimming, travel, plays, movies, eating out, hiking, pickleball, mah jongg, museums and estate sales.

There it was, and there was nothing to worry about, since it appeared the profile could be updated at any time. The last step was to upload a photo. Luckily I had one that my friend had taken just a few weeks before of me hiking. It was a full body shot in which my face was slightly shaded by a cap I was wearing, but it highlighted the leanness of my body. I thought it would impress men with the good shape I was in for a woman my age. My body still looked pretty good with and without clothing. I had adopted her girlfriend's motto: "you don't want to get old and fat, too." Staying trim took most of those mornings in the gym, but it was worth it to feel good and look my best.

With my profile complete I could spend some time perusing the men posting profiles on line. Apparently there were hundreds of men within 75 miles looking for a woman. I had been building a cocoon, isolating myself in my aloneness. It was amazing the number of single men who were looking for a date! I went to bed that night feeling hopeful that I would soon find someone to meet. I didn't want to spend night after night in the company of the dog, TV, or a book, wishing there could be more to life.

Benjamin Book

The number of messages from *POF* the next morning was staggering. I had catapulted from having zero men interested in me to having 104! What an ego booster! There were men who wanted to meet me, men who made me a favorite, men who wanted to flirt and had viewed my profile. I was practically giggling with delight. I eagerly began to read messages from prospects, and profiles from those who had expressed an interest in mine.

One of the first men who really caught my eye was Benjamin Book. He described himself as:

66-year-old man, 5'10", other religion, Caucasian, divorced

Actively seeking a relationship

Intellectual, PhD, retired diplomat

Social drinker, French as a second language

Interested in athletic events, dinners for two

His written description of himself was a bit pompous, but was also enticing. He had written:

I am looking for monogamous passion, a curious mind and ideally at least a college graduate, since I was educated at Stanford and Princeton. I am comfortable and happy, but for lacking a partner to share in my life experiences. I want someone to laugh with, attend the theater, enjoy my exotic fruits, and my passion for cooking. I expect my partner to be the same weight she was in college, assuming she was at a medically correct weight then. If you get your information from TV we probably will not be a good match. I still would enjoy travel for adventure even though I spent my career living abroad.

Benjamin had posted seven pictures of himself, and I was struck by how different he appeared to look in many of them. Major changes happened in a person's appearance past age 60. It was most noticeable in hair color. It was all the more reason to put myself out there while there was still natural color to my hair! I wouldn't have guessed that it was the same man in all of his photos. There was only one really gross one—a full frontal of his upper body that was naked. I could forgive that by the more friendly photos of his smiling face.

I sent off a quick message to him after I found he had marked me as a "favorite". *POF* claimed 40% of all relationships were initiated by women.

Good evening Benjamin,

Your profile is truly unique and I would love to hear more about your career! Your educational credentials are most impressive and I admire those qualifications. I'd like to meet you. We're practically neighbors, since I am on the island, and I too enjoy coffee and conversation. Whenever you'll be visiting the island send a message so we can arrange to meet.

Looking forward to hearing from you,

Katie

The next morning my mailbox showed I had received a reply from him. I eagerly clicked on his message.

Dear Katie,

Your reply to my 'favoriting' you felt great.

Most people are scared off by my very specific profile. We seem to have much in common even though you are Catholic and I am philosophically a Buddhist.

Education is really important although I am somewhat uncomfortable calling myself elite. Many sad experiences have shown I require a female with a cultivated brain and interest in social issues. You appear to be such a person, since you are a lawyer and Catholic.

It's also great that you enjoy hiking and swimming, since there's nothing I enjoy more too.

I am busy this week wrapping up loose ends from my divorce from a woman with ADD, who wouldn't cooperate with court orders. She was also a folie a dieux.

When I can clear my desk I will contact you again. It'll probably be next week.

Ben

I felt a sense of awe and excitement over the prospect of meeting this man who had an enviable career abroad in diplomatic status. He must be really important! It thrilled me that he expressed interest in meeting me. I went off to coffee with my islander friends and had to brag about how I was just on the verge of meeting a retired diplomat who would be so superior to Scott!

It was the right decision to move on —this new man was hundreds of times better educated and interesting than the man I had left behind. His description of his ex-wife being diagnosed as "folie a dieux" did bother me since I'd never heard of it. With my limited command of French I knew that it would briefly translate as "madness of gods" and it wasn't in any medical dictionary. For now, I was willing to let that go.

I got back to the house and even though it had only been an hour since he had written I decided to get right back to him, just to let him know I was seriously ready to meet him, whenever.

Morning Ben,

I'm in from 7 a.m. coffee with the islanders and was glad to see a response from you. As one who dreads dealing with matrimonial matters, which sometimes our office was assigned as pro bono work from the Chief Administrator of the Courts, I can sympathize with the plight you find yourself in today. There was never a divorce that was truly trouble free or without some measure of anguish. I would imagine it may take you some time to recover from this life changing event and gain a true sense of yourself again.

Having grown up in a family in which my parents raised five children, followed by a few years on my own studying at the local university, followed by an engagement then marriage, I was never alone for long. Perhaps that is why I find being alone foreign and am eager to delve into lots of activities to keep myself busy and connected to other people.

It is possible to connect with me via Skype for FaceTime if you're interested in that and have those applications on your computer. Otherwise, I am content to wait until such time as you may have to meet and go exploring.

I would like to know more about why you embrace Buddhism. I think both Buddha and Jesus were extraordinary souls with whom miraculous events occurred. Both began their teachings around age 30, but Jesus came from humble but divine origins while Buddha would have been considered of royal birth. The goal of both was to eliminate suffering and show a way to heaven—perhaps for Buddha a heaven more on earth and within oneself than beyond the physical world we know.

Well, it's obvious I've had my morning coffee. This site isn't too conducive to long replies, so I'll sign off by saying I trust you will be able to sort things out and I will look forward to hearing from you again.

I felt good about our communication and was ready to wait until the following week to talk about getting together. It came as some surprise when, getting back in from the gym, four hours later, there was a reply from Ben. I clicked onto the message.

Katie,

Since you raised such important questions I have the time to answer you immediately. Even though my parents purported to be Christians, my mother was secretly secular and posing as a Catholic.

I was always a free thinker who knew I had to study all religions first in their entirety before I could embrace any one of them. Even though Christianity was a very benevolent societal force, it has become horribly corrupted and thoroughly hypocritical. Christianity, modern science and historical scholarship are in stark contrast to each other. Because I am now a Buddhist, I only say these are my opinions which I would never impose on anyone else.

Since I grew up in the 60s and was a former hippie, I evaluated Eastern religions and found that Hinduism is basically a primitive form of polytheism and animism, and Taoism and Confucianism were not satisfying.

Buddhism is actually two religions: Theravada and Mahayana. Theravada is the old form practiced in Burma, Thailand and Sri Lanka and is only philosophy. Theravada doesn't have gods, saints, sacred writing, clergy or other trappings. Monks will instruct you if you inquire. Buddha is viewed as a human philosopher. This is what I embrace and it is totally compatible with modern science.

Mahayana is a degenerated form of Buddhism practiced in much of the world, including Tibet, China, Japan, and Vietnam. Its multiple gods, saints, prophets, ceremonies, rituals and superstitions and elements of animism and polytheism clearly marks it as a religion.

By comparison, Theravada Buddhism has for its essence self-control, rules resembling the Ten Commandments, and non-binding philosophical writings. For people of intelligence daily meditation is useful. It is highly regarded throughout the world.

I suggest you consult your local library for more books on Buddhism. I do have a large library that you could share.

Ben

I had to read this note over several times in order to digest the gist of it. I was not that familiar with Buddhism except in the most general way and hadn't even known it took two forms. I felt completely inadequate to respond to his message without further thought and consideration, so clicked off of the web as if to pretend I hadn't seen it.

By the next morning, after two cups of coffee, I prepared my response. It would be no use to pretend to know nearly as much as he did so I wouldn't even try.

Good morning Ben,

I very much enjoyed reading your writing on Buddhism and have no doubt about one thing: you are brilliant! Thank you for sharing with me your thoughts on religion. One of the main reasons I practice my faith, which I never struggled to find since it was a gift my parents gave to me, was to make sure to set aside some time to regularly reflect and pray. I have always found it to be of great consolation through good times and, more importantly, bad. I have no doubt there exists a power or energy greater than ourselves, and attempt to imagine what form it may take. We have only ideas, and as Plato thought, ideas may be the only reality we can experience. I find it truly an embarrassment that the Catholic Church is involved in so many scandals which have given good enough cause to many to abandon the faith. But, for me, Christianity is a daily practice, not something that occurs within a building. The world would be a truly marvelous place if people practiced religion instead of warfare.

I was also interested in knowing more about your experience while living with a person with ADD. Was that your first and only marriage? I, too, became involved with a person who lacked focus and exhibited mood swings which were only predictable for their unpredictableness.

It felt like I was riding on a roller coaster. It could be exhilarating but terrifying, passionately exciting then coldly dismissive. The ride became too stressful for my rather quietly passive temperament, but I still sometimes miss the excitement and fun that went with it.

Again, I'm finding it hard to write much in this little box POF provides for messaging. Perhaps you could give me your email or telephone number, or some other way to connect if you'd like to talk to me some more.

I'm happy to be getting company today—my daughter's in-laws have arrived and they will be house hunting around Sarasota/Longboat Key, but will be on the island this afternoon to join me for lunch. When visitors arrive it sets off a flurry of cleaning house so off I go.

I would like to hear more from you. Truly, Katie

It was just over an hour later when my email indicated I had received a new message from Benjamin Book.

Katie,

Even though my marriage lasted 36 years it should have ended earlier. I knew before the marriage that my wife had been institutionalized, but ignored advice from my family to avoid marriage with her. It never occurred to me that such problems would be lifelong. You are right: being with a mentally unstable person is like riding a roller coaster. My now ex never acknowledged having a problem, and she refused any suggestion to seek medical treatment. For the most part she was exuberant but sometimes would turn to a dark and violent side. She could be surly and aggressive, and always anti-social, which is why she was diagnosed with folie a dieux.

My whole family suffered. My oldest son died, and I believe it was a result of her negligence. My other son has turned out to be a successful doctor in the Naples area, having been educated in the Ivy League tradition.

It appears all the loose ends of the divorce are now finalized, even though it took sanctions and costs imposed upon her to act. I think I'm ready to meet you. Name the date and time. Let's get out of this box.

Ben

I pondered the wealth of information provided by his letter. I searched "folie a dieux" again on the web, but could only find a condition called "folie a deux" which was defined as a sort of paranoia in which one person influences a second to experience a shared delusional state. Was Ben the second person in the madness to which he alluded? I was shocked by his accusation that his wife was responsible for their child's death. What a horrible thought! He was obviously hurting and maybe just not even ready to start another long term relationship, even though he said that's what he wanted. Notwithstanding my doubts, I sent a message back to him in the evening. What was the correct way to address a retired diplomat?

Honorable sir,

How about meeting me at Olive Oil Outpost on Pine Avenue tomorrow afternoon at 2? If that doesn't work, then Sunday would work just as well.

I was given a ticket to a local theater production tonight when a friend of a friend left town. It's off to the show for me now.

Please confirm if either option is convenient for you.

Looking forward to meeting you soon.

Katie

I hadn't even signed off the web when his reply was received.

Katie,

It's a done deal. I'll be at the Olive Oil Outpost at 2 p.m. tomorrow to meet you. Remember, my hair is now gray, not the brown shown in my photos. I remember a fairly distant photo of you on your profile. Could you send me a better one to avoid embarrassment? My email is BenB@aol.com. Otherwise just keep a look out for me.

Ben

I went to bed feeling happier than I had felt in ages. Even though it had taken me four messages, over two days, a date was set and it would be the first real date I had since I'd broken up with Scott. Although there had been a walk along the beach with a man I'd met at the gym, that date really didn't count in my mind since I let him know that I wasn't ready to get involved with anyone again just then.

My thoughts turned to what I would wear to the meeting—first impressions were always most important!

First thing in the morning I sent off another note to Ben.

Here we go and have no fear, it's just a cup of coffee, my dear.

You ask how you'll know me; it won't be hard—how many women with a big brown dog can there be?

Another current photo I don't have in ready format; but it wouldn't matter when I'll likely be disguised with sunglasses and a hat.

I'm always early, you'll probably be late; the island tourists have made traffic and parking a sorry state.

I'll be looking for you, and expect you'll be doing the same looking around, too.

And if you see other women giving you the eye, you can say 'My, my, this turned out to be my lucky day!'

There's only seating for a few on the porch, so there will be no need to carry a torch.

When we greet each other it might be best to meet with a kiss on the cheek such as the French like to do, so then we can cross that hurdle in one immediate leap, but that decision is entirely up to you.

See you at two.

I wanted my message to sound slightly melodic, soothing and sweetly inviting. I wasn't quite satisfied with the rhyming pattern but didn't have time to work on it any longer. I was especially pleased with the last line—"See you at two" because it represented our eagerly anticipated introduction, the beginning of what could be a longed for relationship.

The in-laws were stopping by the house to pick me up for dinner at 6 p.m. I had lots of chores to do to straighten up the house to make it look its best. They hadn't been to the island since I bought the house and its remodel was undertaken and somewhat completed, and I hoped they would be impressed by my efforts. I vacuumed and dusted with an unusual energy. I found time to take a dip in the Bay before dressing for the meeting.

I always did arrive early to my appointments; a habit developed over the years of practicing in many criminal courts where clients needed to be soothed and prepped prior to the court calendar being called. The afternoon was beastly hot and I realized hot coffee would be virtually a masochistic choice. My skin was glistening from sweat. Trooper, in an uncustomary manner, was letting me walk in the lead. Whitish drool was dripping from his opened mouth; his tongue hung out in a dejected and surrendering to the heat fashion.

There was no one on the porch of the Outpost. I entered through the beaded curtains that were sufficient to keep the bugs out of the store and I went on into the cool darkness of the shop.

"Do you have some iced coffee today?" I asked the young man behind the counter.

"No, you'd have to go down to Ginny and Jane's for that," he answered.

"Now, young man you should never be too eager to lose a customer. What do you have that's cold?" I asked.

"We have some grapefruit soda that's good," he responded.

"I'll try some of that." I looked around the shop laden with jugs of every imaginable type of olive oil, exotic pastas, crackers and cheeses. The proprietor always set out a plate of crackers and cheese for the customers, but I resisted the urge to try the samples. I felt guilty if I were just getting a drink instead of the more expensive goods for sale in the upscale and unusual shop.

With my bottle of grapefruit soda in hand I went back out to the porch and sat down on one of the six comfy Adirondack style chairs. Trooper was tied to the leg of the chair, and the owner of the shop thoughtfully delivered a bowl of water for him which he lapped up in its entirety. I picked up a copy of the *New York Times* and *Wall Street Journal* set out on a table, to occupy my waiting time. I looked at my watch which showed that it was just about 2 p.m. I glanced over the headlines but found I wasn't able to concentrate on the fine print.

As I stood to stretch I noticed a slender man approaching the porch. He was dressed in khaki shorts, a loose button down shirt and sporting one of those sunhats which was best for blocking the rays of the sun and had straps that could be adjusted under the chin to secure the hat on the head. I had removed my hat, and lifted my sunglasses off of my nose, propping them on my head.

"Ben?" I inquired as the man approached. A smile seemed to cover his face and I leaned forward as he approached me and gave him a peck on the cheek in greeting. His body odor, reeking of sweat, was overwhelming. I quickly stepped back.

"Katie, you were right. I got stuck in traffic," he said.

"It's only to be expected on a weekend here. The island has become almost too popular," I acknowledged sympathetically. "Where did you park?"

"I wasn't sure where this shop was, so as soon as I got on Pine I parked," he said. That explained how he had worked up a sweat—it was probably a quarter mile from the other end of the street. I wondered if I smelled so intensely too, since I had walked over half a mile to get there.

"I decided on a cold drink," I said.

"Let me get myself something to drink," he said. He went inside the shop while I sat down again and occupied myself with *The New York Times*. I had noticed that he had taken no notice of Trooper, who, in his characteristically welcoming way, had also stood up to greet him. He had treated the dog as if the dog did not exist. Ben came out of the shop holding the largest mug of coffee I'd ever seen.

"Can you believe the size of this?" he commented raising the white porcelain coffee mug up for me to admire it, while stepping over Trooper.

"It's a bit warm for something so hot," I remarked. I felt nervous but not especially tense. Ben struck me as a fairly mild mannered man—he hadn't leaned forward to kiss me first. It was easiest to stick to inconsequential remarks until we had both settled into our chairs and became used to each other's company. When some French tourists stopped by to pet the dog as they chattered in their native language it provided some relief from the urge to speak just for the sake of speaking. Ben seemed not to take any notice.

"Ben, tell me more about your career," I suggested.

"Well, I spent 35 years working for the State Department. I was stationed in various foreign countries: Romania, Turkey, and Panama mostly. There was trouble when I was in Panama in the 1989 when the U.S. invaded under Bush's command to remove General Manuel Noriega from power. I was arrested and imprisoned for a time. Noriega had been hand picked by the CIA to assure American control of the Panama Canal," Ben added.

I was having a hard time following his story. I had heard of Noriega but didn't recall the invasion by U.S. troops. I didn't want him to know I was ignorant of U.S. history so I just nodded my head in agreement as he proceeded to list many of the trumped up reasons the government had given to justify the invasion called "Operation Just Cause", including protecting the lives of American citizens, defending human rights, and combating drug trafficking. I was struck by Ben's similarity to my deceased husband in his ability to discourse on a subject at great length with an ease that was akin to delivering a lecture before an auditorium full of college students.

I slowly sipped my soda, wondering how long we'd been there. Trooper remained calm and stretched out under my feet, quietly panting. A small puddle of drool surrounded the area under his snout. Effortlessly Ben continued to talk about the locales he had been assigned. It seemed odd that he made no mention of his wife or family, as if they hadn't even been there with him. It must have been hard for them to move whenever he was given a transfer. I just let him talk, nodding my head every so often, trying to follow his stories and asking questions every so often to clarify or move the history of his career along.

"I'll be heading back to the house soon," I announced, standing and stretching my arms forward. The heat was somewhat subsiding in the midst of a mild breeze blowing east from the Gulf. "The in-laws are coming over to take me out to dinner tonight and I will feel more comfortable being home in case they come early."

"I can walk with you," Ben offered.

I had no qualms about his accompanying me. His conversation in the hours we'd sat together on the Outpost veranda certainly convinced me he was who he said he was and posed no threat to my safety. We headed for the City Pier where I tied Trooper to a post so we could walk out to the pier's end, spotting stingrays and dolphins in the shallow clear waters. At the end of the pier, several hundred feet out into the Bay, we could finally feel cool, swept by the saltwater laden breezes.

We walked slowly under the Australian Pines through the Bayfront Park enjoying the coolness of the shade. Once back at the house I offered Ben a drink. Without hesitation, I showed him the inside of the house and the two types of beers left over in the fridge. He made a grimacing face and mumbled, "Neither," but then reached out his hand and took one.

"Would you like a glass?"

"Sure."

I handed him a glass and fixed a tall glass of iced water for myself. We went outside to sit in the gazebo overlooking the Bay. The heat was so intense bits of black paint were coming off of the wrought iron chairs and sticking to our skin. I was dying to go jump in the Bay, but Ben did not have on a swimsuit, so I didn't mention it. We sat sweltering in the midday sun. One good thing was that Ben never seemed to run out of things to say. In fact, I was finding I barely had to ask a question. He just kept on talking.

Around 6 p.m. the in-laws arrived. Ben seemed content to continue to sit with them and do most of the talking. After another hour they wanted to get going to dinner.

I asked, "Ben, would you like to join us?"

"Yes, how about it?" the in-laws chimed in.

Ben seemed to be at a loss for words. "Well," he mumbled.

"You do have to eat tonight, don't you?" I asked.

"Okay," he said.

Off we walked down the street to the pier, where fresh fish was offered. There was not a long wait for a table, but since the evening breeze was refreshing after the heat of the day, no one would have minded waiting a bit longer on the pier.

When we were seated, Ben continued to do almost all of the talking. We all ordered fish, and I noticed that Ben ordered one of the most expensive entrees on the menu that night—fresh grouper at $27.00. When the food was served everyone but Ben began eating. He continued to talk. As the three of us were nearly finished with our meals I just couldn't stay quiet any longer.

"Ben," I said, "Aren't you going to eat your dinner?"

He finally realized we were nearly done, and began to devour his food with gusto. All of us seemed to finish our food around the same time, but I felt that if I had not ordered Ben to eat, he would have neglected to do so. Perhaps that was how he stayed so slender. No one wanted dessert. When the bill came the in-laws insisted on paying, without any argument from Ben. Ben let them pay for his entire meal! I was taken aback—with his drink, tax and tip, his portion of the bill would have been close to $40.00 and I had just met him a few hours before. Surely he should have insisted on leaving at least the tip! I wasn't impressed. He hadn't made any gesture to contribute his share. We walked back to the house and said our goodnights. The in-laws gave Ben a ride back to his parked car.

Notwithstanding my concern over Ben's lack of etiquette, we spoke the next day and discussed getting together for Memorial Day.

He asked, "What do you want to do?"

"You said you enjoy swimming and kayaking. How I wished we had gone in for an afternoon dip yesterday."

"I have two one-person kayaks," he said.

"That would be great fun," I said. "Trooper presents a problem though. I don't know how long he can be left alone." I was hoping Ben would invite the dog along. He did not.

"I'll have to check with my neighbor who walks him sometimes for me to see if he can help me out." The dog walker charged $10 a walk. Dating had its price. When dog care was arranged, I emailed him.

Hi there good looking,

The fellow who tends Trooper will be able to walk and feed him for me tomorrow afternoon, so I'm good to go.

It appears your place is 36 miles from mine so I'll take the shortcut to Sarasota Airport, then 41 south. Now that dog care has been assured, I'm eager to get an earlier start even if it means lots more sun block may be required. I could leave here about 1 p.m., if that's convenient for you. There will be at least the one stop I'd like to make, since I don't usually get into Sarasota but once a month, or so. There's a Trader Joe's along the route and I'm out of red wine. What is the name of the one you recommended?

I was sorry it did not cool down yesterday afternoon, especially when it seemed that even the wrought iron chairs were melting from the heat of the day. I had my suit on and noticed you wore regular Bermuda shorts. Tomorrow I'd like to swim, and I'll have you know I've been compared to a fish!

When I finally struggled through the crowds to get into the Bay I was rewarded by having a manatee pass by me. I could have reached out to touch it when I remembered that sort of thing is frowned upon. Some woman last year who took a ride on a either a dolphin or manatee was prosecuted. Funny, it seemed, when in many Caribbean resorts swimming with and upon the dolphins is a paid adventure, but one which I never tried.

As far as first dates go, I thought it went well, and I enjoyed getting to know you better. You are a very knowledgeable and informative man whose grasp of most subjects is truly remarkable. I liked hearing about your career. Your stories were fascinating. Are you a member of Mensa International, perchance?

I can understand better why you mentioned that many women were put off by your credentials, which puts you in a class by yourself. I'm not sure you will be able to find me nearly as stimulating. I dread to think of all of the things I have already forgotten since I've lost the need to know them. Speaking French is one example, as well as the intricacies of New York statutes and the common law. My husband was like you--retaining near perfect recall of almost everything he learned-- and he learned quite a bit since reading encyclopedias, law books, as well as ancient Greek and Latin writings, was one of his pastimes. It was always wonderful when he would recite poetry and passages of Shakespeare from memory. In part I thought it was due to the superior method of teaching the Jesuits employed, along with, as you mentioned, having attended top schools. Your intellectual abilities are most impressive, even it they may be a bit intimidating.

I was in communication with the friend I will be visiting in July and she was busy reading <u>A New Earth</u> by Eckert Tolle. She described it as being a mix of Buddhism and psychology, but I was a bit wary when she said Oprah is highlighting the author on her program. Would that be a part of your library?

There's a compelling movie on Netflix entitled 'Into the White,' about British and German soldiers who join forces to survive in the wilds of Norway after their planes were shot down during WWII. That's what I'm up to tonight. See you tomorrow afternoon unless I hear otherwise.

Regards, Katie

When I received his reply not even an hour later I noticed he did what my sister did: he merely inserted his answers in between my text which he somehow copied and pasted from my email, much like a school teacher grading a paper. It was hard to make sense of some of it. He stated:

Katie,

Thanks for the nice warm response. Here are my answers.
--I could leave here about 1 p.m., if that's convenient for you.. There's a Trader Joe's along the route.
Great. I think you might be here about 2:30, or a little later. You can call if things change.

-- I'm out of red wine. What was the name of the one you recommended?
Albero Tempranillo Barrica Organic ($6.99 - buy a bunch)

-- Tomorrow I'd like to swim, and I'll have you know I've been compared to a fish.
I'm looking forward to seeing that.

-- *As far as first dates go, I thought it went well, and I enjoyed getting to know you better. You are a very knowledgeable and informative man whose grasp of most subjects is truly remarkable. I liked hearing about your career. Your stories were fascinating. Are you a member of Mensa International, perchance?*

-- *I can understand better now why you mentioned that many women were put off by your credentials, which puts you in a class by yourself. I'm not sure you will be able to find me nearly as stimulating.*
I really liked our first date, and feel slightly embarrassed that I got a little over wound and talked too much.   Maybe you just turned me on. Certainly you're 'stimulating.'   Despite yesterday, I usually don't talk much about my career (everybody has their moods).   I certainly wouldn't want to try for credentials like Mensa.   But everyone in my family would likely qualify, and probably you.

---*My husband was like you ...*
I was just thinking you mentioned he was in ROTC.   Maybe the recruiting officer felt he didn't need more military training, and told him about the special 2 year program that required no training.

-- *Your intellectual abilities are most impressive, even it they may be a bit intimidating.*
Trust me, your mind and femininity shouldn't allow you to feel intimidated.   You don't need to flatter me.   As you get to know me, you'll see I'm shallower than that ...

-- *I was in communication with the friend I will be visiting in July and she was busy reading <u>A New Earth</u> by Eckert Tolle. She described it as being a mix of Buddhism and psychology, but I was a bit wary when she said Oprah is highlighting the author on her program. Would that be a part of your library?*
No, I don't have this book.   But the link is clear.   Jung and Freud drew on Buddhist psychology to create their new-to-the-West psychiatry.

You might as well go directly to the Buddhist source material.
--See you **Yep.**
Ben

I appreciated that he made mention he thought I was smart too, since I certainly didn't feel like I could keep up with him when it came to discourse. He was so brilliant and talkative I could hardly get a word in! He flattered me with his suggestion that I might be Mensa material. He said he found me stimulating! His comments gave me the confidence I needed to get ready to meet him again.

I got off to a timely start and was glad I had somewhere to go off of the island for the holiday. All the traffic was going in the opposite direction from me—onto the island. I stopped at Trader Joe's and stocked up on red wine, buying the organic blend Ben had recommended as well as the three dollar variety I drank a glass of everyday. Ever since doctors claimed a glass of red wine everyday would do the heart good I had incorporated it into my diet. My father had dropped dead from a heart attack at age 54, his father at age 49, and my oldest sister had suffered a mild heart attack at age 64. At 60, I was well aware of the risk and was glad that now I had a valid reason to have a glass of wine everyday.

I checked in with Ben when exiting the grocery store. "My navigation tells me I'm 20 minutes from you," I reported. "I hope that's about the time we planned." I really couldn't remember what time we had said.

"You're fine," Ben said. "I'm expecting you."

Ben lived in a gated community that featured wide palm tree lined streets, the epitome of the lush tropical climate. His house resembled a Spanish hacienda, with a stucco wall which, over the driveway, had a graceful arched opening. His entire property seemed to represent the jungle Florida once was and it was very impressive. All of his neighbors had similarly overplanted their properties, and it lent a very exotic and lush feel to the surroundings.

He greeted me with an exuberant hug and almost lifted me off of my feet. "Ben, please be careful with your back," I worried. I felt flushed with the pleasure derived from his intense hug.

"Right, I have injured my back before," he said while releasing me from his warm hold.

"Let me show you my garden!" he suggested. He proceeded to take me from tree to tree, bush and flower, naming the plants reverently and mentioning how he had acquired many of them abroad and had started some from seed. I didn't recognize most of the names, even though some trees seemed to be growing a fruit almost identical to a blackberry, and another a raspberry. He picked a small berry from one tree, handed it to me, and said, "I saved this for you."

"Is this what you call lunch?" I said as I popped one berry into me mouth. I noticed that he did not look amused. I hoped he would not expect me to remember the names of his exotic plants because they seemed to be a foreign language I had not yet studied.

"I'll need some help getting the kayaks down and onto the roof rack on my car," Ben said.

"I'm ready whenever you are." We went into the garage where two kayaks were hung from the ceiling, and he began to slowly lower one using a simple but effective pulley system.

"My son hooked up this pulley system," he confessed when I admired how practical and efficient that storage system was. "I'm not any good at household or handy work. I used to just call for a service man," he acknowledged.

We worked together until both kayaks were lowered, carried to his car and lifted onto the roof rack.

"Would you like a coconut juice or soda to have for later?" he asked.

"I'd love to try a coconut juice," I exclaimed. The look he gave me told me I had made the right choice, in his opinion. He took four cans and stuck them into a backpack.

"You should move your car to the street," he said.

"Whatever," I responded but wondered why I couldn't leave it inside the paved courtyard where it would be safely off of the street. There wasn't much traffic in the gated community anyway. I moved my car and asked, "Would you like a breakfast bar from Trader Joe's?" He again made a grimacing face as if that type of food was repulsive.

"Hey, they say they are all organic," I cajoled, until he relented and said, "Okay." I stuck two in my beach bag, along with a towel.

We got into his car and drove to an area for boat launching into the intercoastal waterway. On the way he said, "I can't wait to see you in a bikini." It made me feel uncomfortable. If he actually saw me in a bikini he would be very disappointed. I was wearing a one piece suit that was much more flattering.

He was able to back his car down to the water's edge. We loosened the straps around the first kayak and he began to slide it down the back of the car.

"Darn. Look what that did to my new car!" he said, peering intently at a tiny three-inch, almost imperceptible, scratch. He was very annoyed, and I wondered how that fit in with his avowed Buddhist philosophy which would put very little emphasis on material goods.

"Let's just lift the other one up and off," I suggested.

"Good idea," he said, again complimenting me. The boats were at the water's edge. Ben moved his car to a parking space. I got into the kayak and sat while Ben demonstrated the proper technique for holding the paddle and rowing. I said nothing to the effect that I had paddled before, because I knew I was no expert, having only gone out on Georgian Bay when the waters were at their most calm. He gave me a push into the water and I was off.

Because of the holiday the intercoastal was busy with all types of power boats and kayaks. I followed while Ben led the way across the channel where the power boats had the right of way.

"Now paddle like crazy to cross over before a boat comes charging through and they curse us out," Ben instructed. We waited until the only oncoming boat was a mere speck in the distance. We rowed vigorously until we crossed the channel and entered into a secluded cove. We paddled to a small beach area where many larger boats were docked. I followed Ben in exiting the kayak and hauling it up onto the beach. We removed our things from the waterproof container and stood drinking the cans of cold coconut juice Ben had brought.

"This is absolutely delicious," I said while trying not to gulp down the refreshingly cold drink too quickly. "The bits of coconut are fabulous!"

"I get these at the Asian market for only 12 cents a can," he bragged.

"Take me with you the next time you go," I suggested. The thought of how he had saved money on the meal, at my in-laws' expense, crossed my mind again. He was obviously very conscious of his budget, and not spending much money. We put our empty cans back into the kayak's compartment then climbed up a sand dune. What awaited us on the other side was phenomenally breathtaking. We emerged on the Gulf of Mexico side to a nearly deserted beach. For as far as the eye could see up and down the beach there was no sign of towns or other objects, just plain, gorgeous pristine beach with aquamarine waters lapping onto its shore.

"Where are we?" I wanted to know.

"This is just between Siesta and Bird Key," Ben said. "You can only get here by boat, so not many people can make it."

"Thank you for bringing me here," I said. "This is special."

The waters shone like glistening diamonds forming an undulating blanket, and waves broke into myriads of crystals exploding in the air.

"Let's go!" I said, pulling off my beach cover and running into the surf. I looked behind to see Ben removing his shorts and exposing a pair of vivid red silk swim trunks, which made him look dandy.

Like children we jumped the waves and luxuriated in the refreshing waters.

"Do you know what makes the water this color blue?" he asked.

Oh no, a pop quiz, I thought, but answered, "I always thought it was from the sun and the reflection of the sky."

"There's live algae that influence the color," Ben said. He took some measure of delight in explaining things, and demonstrated the type of mind that was always questioning why things were the way they were. No one would ever call him dull.

We returned to the beach. My towel was spread out on the sand and we sat down on top of it. Our legs touched. Ben leaned over and kissed me. It felt good, comfortable and pleasant. This date was 1000 times better than yesterday's!

He stretched out on his back while I lay on my stomach next to him. He talked about everything and anything. He'd been arrested and imprisoned four times during his career during political upheavals. He'd been offered a full ambassadorship in a small country but his wife didn't want to move again. His son had a good marriage and he appreciated getting to see his grandchildren on weekends.

"Ben, what did you mean by 'folie a dieux?'" I asked. "I never heard of such a thing."

"It's a form a mental illness where two people become delusional." Ben sounded a bit defensive.

"Wouldn't that be 'a deux?'" I asked.

"Oh, so you noticed the spelling," he remarked.

"Who was the second person involved with her mental illness?" I asked.

Ben looked uncomfortable and turned his head away. "There was a woman she spoke to on the phone for hours everyday. They had their own secret life together."

I did not believe him, but didn't want to press the matter further. We were have such a delightful day I hoped it would never end. Soon the heat of the cloudless afternoon began taking its toll.

"I'm going in again," I announced while running into the surf. I dove in and began even strokes swimming parallel to the beach. Ben sat up on the beach and seemed to be intently watching me. I was surprised he didn't join me. I swam until I was tired. I felt a bit insecure as I came out of the Gulf and headed up the dune towards him. He was sitting there watching me still. My sagging thighs were not one of my better parts, and there was no way to hide them. He was still sitting on the towel so I couldn't wrap that around my waist to camouflage them.

"Ready to go?" I asked to divert his attention. The few other people from boats had already left. We were totally alone on this most beautiful deserted beach and I felt at ease with him, almost like he was a brother. It felt safe. We headed back to the other side of the dune where the kayaks were. "They're still here," I remarked. He had expressed some concern about leaving them where they could not be seen and in an unlocked condition. Only someone from one of the boats could have stolen them and they were too big for the boats that had been there to carry them off.

We pushed the kayaks into the water and began a vigorous paddling. Not only were all the other boats gone, but the skies had darkened with rain clouds. As we were crossing the channel, lightning was striking on the other side of the intercoastal waterway. I paddled furiously, afraid of being out in a storm.

"Ben let's get back as quickly as we can. I'm afraid of lightning! Is there any rubber on these kayaks that will protect us?" I asked fearfully. I took the lead and rowed as fast as I could. I stayed ahead of him most of the way back, and pulled the kayak into shore just as light drops of rain began.

Together we lifted the kayaks out of the water and onto the roof of Ben's car. In no time we had them secured with nylon ties. We jumped into the car just as heavy rain began. Back at his house we carefully put the kayaks up to hang in the garage.

"Ben, do you mind if I quickly shower off?" I asked. "I can feel the sand and don't like wearing a wet suit." He showed me through his house and to a guest bathroom adjacent to a guest bedroom. I noticed that the bedroom was furnished with antique carved wooden furniture, much like the stuff I used to collect. I also noticed dirt and dust everywhere. The house was very neat, but the surfaces in the bathroom were stained, and the toilet bowl had turned an ugly yellow. No one had taken a rag to clean anything in months, I thought. The house showed the vestiges of a woman's touch, with some fake flower arrangements and colorful rooms, not something a man would typically do.

"How about some tea?" Ben asked. It was already past 7 p.m.; I'd been with him about five hours, and he'd offered me one exotic fruit that looked and tasted like a blackberry, then a passion fruit which I had scooped out with a teaspoon, for lunch.

"That would be nice," I replied. I was hungry.

The bathroom was equipped with everything needed—soap and shampoo and two dried out looking towels. As I stepped out of the shower/tub combination, I rinsed out the tub and let some remnants of dead bugs, the size of small mosquitoes, wash down the drain. I left it cleaner than I had found it. The toilet had continued to run after it had been flushed. I fixed it by adjusting the ball upward until the water shut off. I used my own wet beach towel to dry myself. The guest towels that were hung on the towel bar were patterned and looked like something a woman would buy. The towels looked stale, like they'd been hanging there for months. I peeked into the medicine cabinet and borrowed some deodorant; I remembered vividly my first impression of him, which wasn't attractive. The cabinet was fully stocked with toiletry items.

The house had a Florida charm, with high ceilings and ceiling fans spaced every few feet. He had mentioned that he thought it was worth about $400,000, and he would know since it had just been the subject of a division of assets in his divorce proceedings. It looked like it would sell for a million dollars, but I really didn't know what values were in these interior gated communities. The exterior courtyard was a gem, with an ornate water fountain that could double as a small pool in the center and a corridor that was enclosed by a ceiling, circling around the center. It had the feel of a monastery. Someone had thoughtfully installed a five-foot high white fence around the fountain to keep children away from the water, which looked garish, but necessary with little ones. If it had been my house I would have removed the fencing when the little ones weren't about. But, it did look like the last thing on Ben's mind was the appearance of his living conditions.

When I entered the kitchen, with an island in the middle of the open space, he was standing next to the stove. A water kettle was set on the stove to boil. He had set out two mugs on the tiled counter. I picked up the yellow mug with a smiling face on it. "I'll use this one. Psychologists say that if you smile more often you'll actually feel happier," I remarked. His face had a somewhat blank expression on it and he made no comment to the psychological tidbit on being happy.

"Did you have time to shower?" I asked.

"No, I just sprayed on some cologne. Would you like mint tea or green?" Ben asked.

I recoiled at the prospect of covering up sweat with cologne, even though I too had been known to do that. I wanted to say "neither" to the offer of tea, since the evening was still quite humid and something hot to drink was not going to feel refreshing. Suddenly he approached me and waved his hands in front and across my face as if he were slapping me.

"Decide!" he ordered. I took a step back and felt uncomfortable by his gesture. I remembered he'd mentioned his ex-wife could become violent. Maybe he was used to being slapped. Soft rain was making music on the roof overhanging a narrow lanai.

"Green will be fine," I replied. He leaned forward, took me in his arms, and gave me a long slow kiss. His cologne smelled good, subtle but not overpowering, but I would have preferred the scent of clean skin. The kiss might have gone on forever if the tea kettle hadn't started whistling.

"You know you could live here," he said out of the blue.

Ben poured the boiling water into the cups, and we stood near the kitchen island counter waiting while it seeped.

"What kind of diet do you like," I asked pointedly, changing the subject, since it was getting quite late and we hadn't eaten.

"I lost 30 pounds quickly last year eliminating white from my diet."

"A lot of people are doing that. It's not easy though to forego sugar, flour, rice and other bread and pastries," I acknowledged. I now dared not ask for the sugar I liked to have in my cup of tea.

"I stay on the Mediterranean diet now. I enjoy cooking and could cook you a meal sometime," he said.

I wished he would try out his cooking skills on me right then. It had been six hours since I had arrived, and all I had was a berry or two, a scoopful of passion fruit, a can of coconut water and the breakfast bar I had brought. I thought of the expensive meal he had been provided and was annoyed.

He led me out a table for two on his screened in lanai overlooking a small pond surrounded by natural foliage. It was very peaceful with the rain gently dancing on the overhang, and I felt like I would be content to just sit with him there for many more hours. In the middle of the table he had placed a small bowl. In it there were some dates, figs, cashews and one piece of chocolate. I tried a cashew and was surprised to find it flavored with a piquant flavoring. I took a fig and then a date, chewing on them slowly to savor the experience of eating.

"Try the chocolate," he suggested.

"Would you like half of it?" I asked, holding up the one inch square. He said nothing so I popped the whole thing into my mouth. I stopped eating since he was not eating. I was determined not to look too hungry no matter how ravenous I felt. When my cup of tea was drunk I remembered I had to get home to Trooper, who was supposed to have been fed and walked around 5 p.m., which would mean, calculating in the hour it would take to drive home, that the dog would need to be let out again upon arrival. I excused myself and stood up to leave.

"Think about what you want to do next," he suggested, taking me into his arms and holding me close. He seemed to be answering his question. I reluctantly pulled away from him, picked up my bag and made my way to the door. He accompanied me out to my car, kissed me again for the road, and off I went.

The next day I felt confused and uncertain about how things were progressing with Ben. He was moving very fast and I was not sure I was ready to jump into such an intense relationship after just two dates, both of which exhibited some signs with which I was not comfortable. Would I have felt differently if he had taken me out to eat, reciprocating in kind for the treatment he had been given? Maybe, but maybe it was more that we had not spent the time in public places which would have made me feel more secure about him.

At coffee with my friends, the women were amazed that we hadn't eaten dinner after seven hours together.

"When he asks you what you want to do, tell him you want to eat!" suggested my sympathetic friends.

"It's not a good sign that he doesn't want to take you out," my dear friend Jane insisted. "Part of the getting-to-know each other process involves how you relate in public situations."

I had to agree. Things were just moving too fast for me. By the third date Scott and I had become passionate and inseparable and it hadn't given us the time to get to know each other in typical social settings, which would have alerted me to many of his character quirks, which ultimately led to our demise. I did not want to repeat that experience. I may be old, but I wasn't desperate, and thought it would be wiser and involve less heartache in the long run to take a bit longer to get to know someone.

I let the week go by without calling him, nor did he call me until the next weekend. When I answered the phone and heard his sedated voice I sensed he was somewhat miffed with me.

"Ben, I needed to take some time to think things over. It felt like everything was going too fast for me."

"That's okay," Ben said. "I find you very attractive and hoped we could work towards the long term relationship we both want."

"I'm not sure I'm ready to commit with you. When my prior boyfriend wanted to live and travel together he gave me a ring as a sign of his affection and commitment to me."

Ben seemed to explode in anger. "You've got to be kidding! Didn't you read my profile carefully! I made it clear I would never give anyone material items again."

I was astonished by the intensity with which he spoke, and tried to remember what his profile had said. I could recall something to the effect of not putting emphasis on material items. He hadn't seemed to have felt that way when it came to scratching his new car.

"Ben, it's just that if I ever want to introduce you to my family I feel we have to admit our devotion to each other, that's easiest shown by a sign."

"We can be devoted and share a monogamous relationship without marriage. I will never get married again, and no divorced man ever wants to get married," he asserted in a loud and angry way.

"I don't know about that," I said. "I've known lots of divorced men who remarried."

"You could try to talk me into it;" he said, and then with a sudden change of mind again insisted, "no, don't even think it. I will never marry you and I will never give you a ring."

"Did you try to talk your son out of getting married?" I countered. "I'm not afraid of commitment or eventually taking a public vow of a lifelong commitment," I said.

"Katie, you must go onto your profile and edit it to reflect that you want to get married. It's not right that you are indicating you want a long term relationship."

"But I'm not ready to get married again. I just want to leave open that as a future possibility with someone I'm dating."

"It's never going to happen with me," Ben insisted again.

"Thanks for talking to me Ben. Goodbye," I said as I hung up the phone.

I was visibly shaking by the intensity of the communication. It felt like he'd been yelling at me and I felt drained by the emotional exchange. I was grateful our views were out in the open and exposed such differences in our values, before they had let our association go any further.

It was easy to break off with someone whom you knew for only for a week, and with whom you have not been intimate.

Diamonds4u

I carried on with my routine and met the islanders for coffee at 7 a.m. the next morning. A quick look at my calendar when I got back to the house after coffee reminded me that had my husband lived we would have been celebrating our 35th wedding anniversary that day. I checked in online. There was a new message waiting for me from *POF* from Diamonds4u. I clicked onto the message center to view it, which had just been written at 8 a.m. that morning.

Hello neighbor

I see you faved me

Thanks for the vote of confidence

Do you have a picture to share?

Hugh

I was struck by how cute his username was—a real imaginative and appealing one at that! What woman didn't want diamonds as a symbol of her man's love for her? After what Ben said was his position concerning material items like rings, it was nice there was a traditional man out there who still believed in things like giving gemstones to his woman. I really couldn't remember having "faved" him, so checked my list and saw that he was one of about four profiles during those first days online that I had marked as "favorite" in order to remember to review it again. I had gotten busy with Ben and forgotten all about everyone else. I didn't even know then the user would receive notification of it. I reviewed his profile:

Widowed 57-year-old, Catholic, seeking a relationship

Class Clown personality, Longboat Key, Bachelor's degree, retired

Black hair, blue eyes

longest relationship over 10 years

Interested in love at first sight, keeping you laughing,

kissing, adventure, sports

When I read his *Description* I remembered why I marked him as a favorite. He seemed perfect, albeit three years younger. More importantly, the man was hilarious! He wrote:

I've had a fabulous life in the entertainment business presenting famous artists.

I'm not your typical shallow internet date.

I'll maintain my morals unless you insist otherwise.

I don't understand atheists, creation and people who don't like me.

I don't like POF women who fave you but make no effort to meet.

I believe in love at first sight.

I would live anywhere for just the right kiss.

We'll be busy on our first date getting your fingerprints checked out at the sheriff's office, and checking for hidden weapons. It's after the first date that things will be fun.

Beware gold diggers—I am an expert at spotting you.

I imagined that he must be a comedian who introduced the main act, like those live shows in Las Vegas. He had posted several photos, some with people who were presumably famous, two good close ups and another odd one in which he appeared to be in some weird costume. Overall he looked handsome and wholesome. I wrote back:

My picture was somehow deleted, but just for you will try again! I'm too busy laughing over your post to write more now.

An hour later another message was received from Hugh.

When you subside to a workable giggle think about when we can meet at Joe's for an ice cream . . . or root beer float.

How very sweet and appealing Hugh sounded. How convenient it would be to have a boyfriend just down the road, so to speak. The drive out to Ben's took close to an hour yesterday, and this was in low season and off peak hours. It could easily take twice that long when the snowbirds and tourists came flocking to the area. I took off for my morning at the gym and felt better when my friends agreed that Ben was not worth pursuing. Of course, since most of the pickleball players were long married people, they didn't have the perspective that someone who was divorced would have. I wore myself out playing pickleball, going for a swim afterward and running Trooper several miles until he was thoroughly exercised. I went to bed exhausted.

In the morning I remembered Hugh. I sat down at my computer and shot off an early morning message to him.

Hello Hugh,

I've never met anyone who characterized himself as a clown—it must be hard to remain the funniest man in town.

You say you believe in love at first sight? Who needs a date then, we can just arrange for a drive by, but hopefully not at night!

How exciting your interests include a bit of kissing; there's something that I have longtime been missing.

A typical shallow internet date I too wouldn't buy, but since I don't know what that is I'm willing to give it a try.

After I pass inspection at the police station and you find my fingerprints come back clean, will you be willing to undergo the same screen?

I can meet you at Joe's wherever that is, and whenever you say, but with appointment required since I try to stay busy most everyday.

So let's leave it at this and that, until you suggest a more definite time to continue this chat.

Tuesday after three would work for me.

But it will have to be a diet soda or Italian ice for me; otherwise you might think I'm not that nice to see.

I sent off my reply without much notice of the fact that it had been written in rhyme. It just seemed to have happened that way without any effort, but I was pleased with my communication and hoped he found it cute and funny too. He must have found it agreeable because later that morning he messaged back:

The location of Anna Maria has always confused me because of local signage. If you never heard of Joe's ice cream place then you must be at the northern tip. If you head south on the trolley you will pass Manatee then Cortez and a block past Bridge Street on your left you'll see Joe's.

Tues. at 3:45 I should be getting off my trolley and heading to Joe's once I grab my bike off the front.

That places me at Joe's by 3:50.

If the trolley is late I'll complain to the Mussolini running the schedule.

I'll bring plenty of comedy material and a few props if I can at least find a whoppy cushion that hasn't melted.

If you get there early you can check me out on my bike drive-by.

I'll wait for the thumbs up before my dismount.

What say you?

Ready for a comic relief chapter in your memoir?

Hugh

I was flushed with pleasure from reading his response and laughed at the thought of his arriving by bicycle after he transported it on the local trolley. I loved the way he was able to make a jab at the local government without saying anything nasty. His sense of humor just shone through everything he wrote! When he suggested he'd wait until I gave him the thumbs up it seemed as though he were being quite considerate. I didn't know what a "whoppy cushion" was though and wondered if he would actually show up with props, and if that was a normal part of his comedy act. He must have been quite famous in places like Vegas, I mused. He was very self-confident and must have had the good sense to retire while he was still very young and just enjoy the money that a profession like show business would earn. To think, first I got to meet a diplomat who was a bit of a drone, but fascinating nonetheless, and now I was going to meet someone much more famous than that and fun too! I reveled in my good fortune, and shot off a quick response to Hugh.

I, like you, will head for the trolley by bicycle at three,

But who knows exactly when it will deliver me at Joe's for you to see.

I'll be disguised in sunglasses and hat,

Which, if you lead me to someplace shady, I may remove for our chat.

So don't despair if I may be late,

You'll know the culprit to berate.

You might want to provide a number to contact you by cell,

So you can rest assured I'm not telling you to go to hell.

Ten minutes later, Hugh sent his reply:

Ooohh,

I got so excited until I spotted the comma after 'I'

I have punctuation issues

See you there

I doubt you'll be needing to use the H E double hockey sticks at our meet

Hugh. . . 941-214-0526

There was another reference I couldn't follow. What were H E double hockey sticks? I figured he just must be implying that I wouldn't need anything to defend myself with for our date. Hockey sticks could be used as a defensive weapon I supposed. It was only noon, and I had a whole day to anticipate meeting Hugh. Even though he struck me as being rich and famous, and in fact, certainly alluded to that status in his profile, I was not too nervous about the meeting. After all, it was just a casual drink at a local ice cream parlor, just a few miles down the road, in the middle of the afternoon.

In the morning I got up and going, bragging to the women at coffee how I was meeting someone quite renowned in the afternoon. They all were eager to hear the details. In a way, my efforts to meet men and date were getting to be the local entertainment. When I checked my email, the following message had come in while at the gym:

"So unless Trooper is acting up and becoming the culprit for cancellation of our ice cream social. . . I will continue to prepare for our rendezvous this afternoon. Hugh

I liked how Hugh incorporated the dog humorously into his text, which showed he had really tried to get to know me from my profile. He made our meeting seem exciting and I felt certain the afternoon was going to be fun. I wrote back after getting dressed to go, wanting to provide him with a sense of what I did everyday:

7 a.m.: coffee with islanders—check

8 a.m.: housework—check

10 a.m.: pickleball at gym—check

Noon: lunch—check

1 p.m.: run Trooper 2 miles—check

2 p.m.: shower and decide to wear swimsuit to first date—check

3 p.m.: ride bike to trolley stop—in progress

3:50p.m.: fall in love at first sight with Hugh—

Before leaving on bike for the trolley, his message was received:

Now if only both of us cooperate in getting your list accomplished!

This man was entirely likeable and fun! Over my one piece v-necked black swimsuit I wore a white cotton beach cover up with a zipper down the front and a hood which I could pull up to protect my head from the sun while riding, but wouldn't plaster my hair down on my head. I left for the trolley stop at the pier and only had to wait a few minutes before the trolley arrived. The driver helped hoist the bicycle on the front of the trolley, and off I went.

Since I had caught the 3 p.m. trolley and it got half way to the destination within ten minutes, I exited the trolley at the Manatee Public Beach stop and proceeded to ride the rest of the way. I pulled into the parking lot of the ice cream parlor by 3:30 p.m., looked around for another bike, and when I saw none proceeded to bike around the area killing time until it was our meeting time. I returned to Joe's on schedule and sat on the elevated open porch which had a small view of the Gulf of Mexico across the street. Very few people were riding bikes in the heavily trafficked area. I sipped on the bottled water I always carried, and watched a young overweight couple at the adjacent outdoor table finish their ice cream and depart.

I stood up to walk over and claim the vacated table, which was closer to the edge of the porch looking over the Gulf. As I was beginning to move I saw a striking man appear at the top of the stairs. He had an easy gait and could have passed for anywhere from 40 to 60, that middle age period when noticeable changes in appearance still haven't emerged. He appeared to be smiling at me and my instinct was to move closer to him. He pushed the sunglasses he was wearing up to the top of his head and I could see he matched the photos on *POF*.

"Hugh?" I asked as I extended my hand which he took in his. He brought my hand up towards his mouth and I thought he was going to kiss it. That type of greeting was very romantic indeed. Instead, as my hand, which he continued to hold in his, approached his mouth, he leaned forward and kissed not my hand, but his own instead. I had to chuckle a bit, which was, no doubt, his intention. As we stepped back and away from each other I gave him a once over and liked what I saw even though I was disappointed that he did not show up for our date wearing a swimsuit after I had told him I would. After all, the Gulf beckoned right across the street. Then I remembered that he

47

mentioned he owned Gulf front property, so it was no big deal to him. He wore a loosely fitted brown button down shirt, casual slacks and brown leather loafers. He looked simply and casually elegant. We stood looking at each other almost eye-to-eye.

"You are quite the catch," he said.

I stepped back and with utmost seriousness asked, "Are you feeling anything yet?" making an oblique reference to his interest in falling in love at first sight. He didn't seem to get it. "Do you want to sit outdoors or go inside?" I asked.

"Let's go inside," he answered.

We moved towards the door, which he leaned forward and opened for me. He was a gentleman. We stepped inside and stood before the counter peering up at the menu board behind it. I certainly was not going to have ice cream, but spotted a refrigerator with sodas and a popcorn machine filled with freshly popped brightly colored yellow corn.

"I think I'll have a diet soda and a small popcorn," I said.

"I'm going for the root beer float," Hugh said. I hadn't known anyone to like root beer floats since a neighbor claimed them as a favorite, decades ago. He fumbled in his pocket and pulled out a brown leather billfold. Removing a $20 bill he said, "Wait, I have some change I brought to get rid of." Slowly he counted out the amount of change in coins and pushed them across the counter. I just stood quietly next to him. I felt a certain calm undercurrent and it felt good. I made no offer or effort to pay.

"You are starting a precedent here," I remarked as the clerk took his money. But it was a cheap date, I thought to myself, having set him back only a couple of dollars. We walked into what appeared to be the dining area, two rows of tables for four set in front of a large picture window that captured the view of the Gulf of Mexico. Only one other table had people around it so we chose another table set apart a bit and sat down enjoying relative privacy in an otherwise public spot.

Immediately I recognized I had made a <u>big</u> mistake in ordering the popcorn. I should have just stuck with the soda. It was greedy to go for more than I really wanted. It seemed every other handful of popcorn left some falling out of my hand and dropping onto my clothes or the table. I scooped up the fallen corn in embarrassment and then did not know what to do with the kernels, so just pushed them into a little pile on the table that grew in size as the date progressed. Since he sat just a few feet away from me across the table it was impossible for him not to notice. Once, when one dropped out of my mouth, he turned his head away with his lip curled a bit as if he found having to watch me eat a bit disgusting. Sensing this, I scooped up the dropped kernels, stuck them back into the bag and folded the paper down. The trying-to-eat popcorn spectacle was over.

His demeanor was really quite debonair. He sat calmly and confidently, speaking softly.

"Please tell me more about your years in the entertainment industry," I asked.

He looked at me somewhat blankly. "I was a promoter, that's all," he said.

I wasn't sure what a promoter was and was a bit afraid to ask, thinking this was something I ought to know, but stupidly didn't. Then, realizing I was still licensed to practice law, I could afford to look stupid if I wanted. "Tell me more," was all I could come up with.

"Well, I basically backed new acts," he explained. Unfortunately, his explanation failed to paint much of a picture, but of one thing I felt certain—he was putting up money for up and coming entertainers.

"I just got back from Vegas last week," I remarked. "In the mornings my brother and I would go hiking and in the afternoon we would take in one or two shows. Some of the shows were extraordinary. The Cosmopolitan featured entertainment that rivaled Cirque de Soliel."

Hugh nodded his head in agreement as if he'd been there and done that. "Yes, the Red Rock Canyon is fun for hiking," he agreed.

"Hugh, you really had me fooled though. I just assumed that since you were so humorous you must be a comedian! I can't believe how wrong I was about you. How long have you been widowed?" I asked.

"It's been four years. My wife died in my arms," he remarked.

"It must have been tragic," I commented sympathetically.

"She died from excesses in drugs and alcohol," he told me. "Before her I was divorced from a woman whom I had been married to for 29 years, and with whom I had two children. My second wife and I did not have any children. She had one son, but I never see him anymore."

I was impressed with the amount of information he shared with me, and noted that his first marriage had been of long term. The thought occurred to me that if his second wife had been using drugs and alcohol there was a chance that he had too. "My husband was an alcoholic," I told him, "but he died from cancer. I go to alanon meeting on the beach every week."

"I do too," he said.

"I've never seen you there," I remarked. I wondered if he were over on the other side of the beach where the alcoholics and drug addicts met. He looked completely sober and in control of all of his faculties. Maybe Longboat had its own beach meeting.

"After my husband died I had one boyfriend, for a year and one-half," I volunteered.

"What happened?" Hugh asked.

"He was Canadian so it was a bit of a long distance romance," I related. "I left him nine months ago because our temperaments were so different. He was very emotional. I wouldn't go so far as to say he was bipolar, but he was probably borderline. It felt like I was riding on a roller coaster with him and it all became too stressful for me. He would be intensely passionate, then suddenly coldly dismissive." I couldn't believe I was spilling my guts to this good looking stranger, but the words were just pouring out.

Hugh sat shaking his head in agreement. "What, no baby after nine months?" he joked. "I know exactly what you mean about the roller coaster ride," he said without further elaboration.

Then, not knowing what got into me, I volunteered, "my boyfriend was impotent, as was my husband for the last years of our marriage." My intent was to let him know he did not have to worry about sexually transmitted diseases with me, but it came out more like a confession and I couldn't figure why I mentioned it.

"You are long overdue," he exclaimed softly in a jocular manner. His eyes were soft.

"I can't believe I just told you that," I said, with the emphasis on "just".

"What do you miss?" he asked with a dry wit, although I interpreted it as a real question.

"I miss living with someone. I came from a family of five children, then spent a few years at the local university where a girlfriend and I shared a house off campus. After graduation I met my husband. We got engaged, lived together a bit and were married shortly after that. I never really lived alone for long and find it almost unnatural." I stayed quiet on the different techniques used to get sexual thrills.

Hugh seemed to be listening intently and with a sympathetic ear.

"I miss sleeping with someone," I confessed.

"Your place or mine?" Hugh asked teasingly. I sat mute. Was he serious? Did people really go to bed with each other on the first date these days? I thought that must be craziness, but I knew nothing. Did he think I was asking for it since I elaborated on my sexual history?

"You know, you would be a younger man for me. I'm three years older than you are," I said.

"No, I'm really 61," Hugh replied. "I just put that so when women are searching they won't automatically rule me out because I come in at the over 60 age category."

I appreciated his honesty, and thought he could pass for younger than 57. I wondered if he colored his hair or had any cosmetic work done.

"Tell me more about what you do," I asked pointedly changing the subject.

"I deal in diamonds," he said. Maybe that's how he chose the username "Diamonds4u" I thought. "I like to go to estate sales. I buy the stuff there and then consign it for resale. If I'm in doubt I have a friend who can appraise more accurately than I can."

"I like sales too," I said. "I have a sister who goes sailing every weekend. I used to say I went tag saling."

Pulling off the diamond from my right hand ring finger, I handed it to him and said, "Tell me what you can about this."

He took the ring and held it some distance away from his face. "It looks like its set in platinum."

"Yes, it is platinum," I said.

"It looks like it could be five carats," he continued then extended the ring back to me

"My father-in-law gave it to me when I passed the bar examination in New York. I always wondered what it was worth," I said.

"I lived in Buffalo for many years," Hugh said.

"I stopped in Buffalo last year and was impressed by how much the downtown was up and coming. I saw the Frank Lloyd Wright house and it was amazing! But, the best thing about Buffalo is leaving it," I said. Then, realizing that it may have sounded demeaning to his home town, I continued, "There's a route, I think it's route 5, that travels south along Lake Erie from Buffalo. It's quite scenic and shows the great old houses along the lake."

"Yes, that's it," Hugh said.

"I lived outside of New York City on Long Island for the most part for the last 34 years," I continued.

"I used to fly into New York by private plane to meet with clients on a fairly regular basis," he said. It certainly sounded like he was very rich indeed. He looked it too, in a richly understated way. There was nothing flashy about him.

I hadn't worn a watch but felt a kind of stiffness from sitting in one chair for a long time. He seemed to sense my discomfort, and made a shifting motion in his chair like he was ready to stand up as well.

"I really thought we'd be taking a walk on the beach," I said.

"Oh, the Gulf's in my backyard," he reminded her, since he'd put that in his post. "I have several properties and may sell. I sold $50,000 worth of AT&T from my trust this morning."

Again, I sat quietly not knowing how to respond. He offered several different types of information. One, he had a trust agreement which might indicate that his money was somewhat insulated and protected. Second, selling $50,000 worth of stock was a commonplace occurrence for him. But then, was the money meant to last him a week, a month, three months, a year?

"I always considered AT&T a rock," I commented. "I knew many people who made small fortunes from it, especially shortly after its monopoly was broken up into the baby bells." I didn't mention that I kept 5% of my portfolio in AT&T stock which paid a healthy dividend of 5% annually.

"Well, I remember one of the baby bells not doing so well," he replied.

I looked out the window and commented, "It's always so calming to gaze out over water." Hugh stood up signaling that our date at Joe's was over. I gathered up my soda can and leftover popcorn and tossed them into the trash can. Immediately I was sorry that I hadn't checked to see if the place recycled. I was so good about recycling at home; it would be a shame to give the impression that I didn't care about the environment, by not engaging in activity that protected it in little ways. It was too late now.

We exited the parlor and he followed me down the rickety wooden steps to my bicycle I had dropped under the elevated porch. "I saw your bike when I pulled in," he said.

"I got it from a pawn shop for $25, and never need to worry about it being stolen," I explained. "I only biked half way," I confessed.

"I was running late so just jumped into the car," he responded.

"You'll have to end this," I said. "I don't know how."

He stood just a few feet away facing me and his eyes seemed to be exploring mine. He stepped closer and took me into his arms, encircling my waist and pulling me closer to him. I put my arms around his shoulders and lost myself in the comfort of his touch. He felt good. "You are soft," he whispered. I could have stayed in that hugging position indefinitely. I felt his leg sway against mine and I pulled away.

"Thank you Hugh," I said, hopping onto the bike and beginning to pedal away. I turned to watch him walk towards a white vehicle that resembled a jeep, and open the door. I gave him a jaunty wave goodbye. He reciprocated in kind.

I biked half the way home and again, then caught the trolley. I would have continued on bike, if the afternoon hadn't gotten so hot. I never did jump into the Gulf. Once home I sat to reflect on what had happened, realizing that nothing was said about meeting again. Maybe it had been an interview and I had not, in effect, gotten the position although I was treated with due consideration. Or maybe he just wasn't thinking about the next date while we were still on the first one. Dating was still so new that I didn't know what to think.

The next day I did my thing at the gym and spoke to my friends about the gazillionaire who offered to take me to bed on the first date. They were amused. Did men think women just wanted to jump into bed with them without a bit of wining and dining? Obviously. I was still wondering what current dating etiquette was when it came to follow up. I knew one thing: I'd like to see him again.

Two days post date I decided the best approach was to just tell Hugh I enjoyed our date and would like to see him again. It was preferable to waiting for some type of communication from him. I sat down at the computer in the morning, and a message wrote itself:

There were some really good things about our first date

that I'd like to mention so thought I would state,

to which I was hoping you could relate.

My first impression of you I can honestly tell,

your looks, physique and demeanor I found to be swell;

and it was a relief you showed up as well.

As you approached me from the top of the stairs on Joe's porch,

my delight with our meeting should have shone like a torch.

I excitedly rose to greet you, feeling something like bliss;

never shall I forget your unique first kiss!

It was hard not to stare at your smoothly coiffed black hair,

the bit around the ears, of gray, was the only hint of giving your age away.

Your blue eyes were soul searching and deep;

and what a joy it could be to see them last before sleep.

You were softly spoken, with each word at ease;

and it was obvious, with women, you knew how to please!

I was really embarrassed I had sloppy popcorn to eat,

getting the kernels in my mouth turned out to be no easy feat.

How I wished I'd ordered instead something sweet.

It felt like with you I was wearing a smile,

and I could have stayed on with you for awhile;

not having long to bike a far mile.

If ever you want to hear more, just drop me a line;

which is all that's needed to give me a sign.

Where ever we meet next together would be fine;

you might even one day show me the way to cloud nine.

This is just so you know I don't view our encounter as some silly game;

even though I am wishing I could remember your full name.

Never shall I forget your unique first kiss.

I sat back and was pleased with the message. I hoped Hugh would find it similarly light and airy, fanciful and fun. Somehow when I pressed some buttons the line "Never shall I forget your unique first kiss" was copied and pasted onto the bottom of the rhyme, which I didn't even notice until afterward. There really hadn't been a first kiss—he had kissed his own hand instead of mine, and that I remembered.

Within minutes, I heard the welcome ding of a message coming in. I clicked on it eagerly and was very pleased to see it was from him.

Sorry doll

We had a spectacular hug but you never delighted me with a kiss

Had we done that we might have been waking up together at least by the weekend

Busy today?

I laughed at his brazenness. This was obviously a man who was enjoying his widowerhood and having his way with women. Regardless of his profile's stated intent to form a long term relationship, I wondered if he were enjoying more the dating process in getting there. He certainly was confident, and I went off for my morning at the gym feeling somewhat delighted nonetheless.

When I got back in the afternoon the following message was drafted in reply:

Now that I've heard from you

I find myself suddenly free!

If you'd suggest a place for we two

to meet later today, we could soon see.

But beware my internet man, dear

for one thing should be made clear. . .

Before any man took me off to his bed,

it was as if, you could say, we were nearly wed.

It was a struggle deciding whether to say "nearly wed" or "near wed" then it seemed it didn't make a difference. The point was if I were going to bed with someone it was akin to being married to that man. Like Ben, Hugh seemed to be moving very fast and I wondered if all that much had changed in the past 35 years. I had very limited experience, but always assumed people got to know one another a bit more before becoming intimate. It was looking like I was wrong about that. I sent off my reply and occupied myself with household chores, which I seemingly danced through.

Two hours late a quick message from Hugh was received:

Off to bed? . . . but I'm not even tired

Did you want to take a dip in the ocean?

I really did want to go swimming with him. Within the hour I wrote back,

I always enjoy dipping in the ocean,

As long as I'm wearing lots of lotion.

Do you want to set a time and a place

Where we can again meet face-to-face

I clicked off of the internet, then, in eager anticipation, proceeded to back a beach bag, apply sun block, and put on my sexiest swimsuit. Trooper was fed and taken out for a long run. Upon my return there was the following message:

Let's see what the weather does. . . .

Weekends are usually busy.

I was dumbfounded. Here I was, packed and practically out the door and his message not only was putting me off, but letting me know that he wouldn't be able to see me this weekend either. I immediately thought this must be because he had another girlfriend or else why couldn't I theoretically spend time with him? The weatherman had predicted some lightning and thunder; the skies were dark but the storm never materialized. I unpacked my bag and poured myself my daily five ounce glass of red wine. I really didn't understand men, but did think I knew when one was dismissing me.

The next morning I drafted another query to Hugh, because I wanted him to know I was really interested in him. I had hoped to hear from him but nothing more had come in.

I titled it, *How about You?*

Would you reconsider a second date

with one you hadn't heard from of late?

When I think of you I'm moved to rhyme,

you're a tune with a pleasing melody,

a poem that resonates in my mind;

something I'd like to hear, see and feel another time;

you move me, Hugh, to the sublime.

If nothing else we can compare our notes,

to see which POF candidates would get our votes.

No matter how I revise my profile to attract just the right men,

There you appear, Diamonds4u, number one among my top ten!

Can a computer program so much smarter than me be wrong?

Why else would just thinking of you make me want to write you a song?

Give me some advice on what you think I should do;

to finish with this program and be all the way through.

Maybe I gave you the impression I'm some kind of prude,

and it's not my intention to sound somewhat rude,

but there are more imaginative ways to meet the heart's need for food;

without saying more, else it might sound quite lewd!

Oh wonderful nourishment that may come from just our first kiss;

joy and promises of rapture with you I wouldn't want to miss.

If you have reasons you'd rather not hear from me;

(I'm not witty, rich, young, beautiful, talented, skinny enough to see, e.g.)

I'll know from your silence you hit the delete key.

I sat a long time looking over the note, but then decided not to send it. It was saved it to my drafts.

I hadn't given Hugh my phone number so I didn't have to sit around thinking he might call, which was actually a tremendous relief.

The islanders, who had become my ad hoc advisory board, kept warning me to guard my private information, as well as not allow any first dates into the house, and they were right.

Haiku4u

To take my mind off of the Hugh dilemma, I decided, considering what Ben had said about my misleading men by not disclosing my belief in marriage, I should revise my profile. I clicked onto *POF* and went to *Edit Profile*. In another click of a button I was able to change my *Intent* to "wanting to get married" instead of "looking for a relationship" and the *Headline* from "Let's Talk" to "Expecting Lightning to Strike and Wanting Miracles!" I deleted the prior *Description* of myself and wrote something new, still feeling the sting of Ben's angry words.

If you've gotten past the 'wanting to marry' intention you are a courageous man indeed!

Do you feel old when it comes to love? I don't, although with all of the choices this website has to offer it could be that meeting the right man to enjoy life with will be a miraculous event indeed. We have to become innocent and vulnerable again, opening our hearts to the possibility of erotic love and believing that just the right person exists for us. No matter that we may be entering the last third of our lives, we can retain youthfulness that being young-at-heart will give.

Being out in the single and ready-to-date scene seems not too different from those first encounters with romance. What have we learned? I think we have to meet each other first, date a bit before we can form a relationship, and from there we might enter into a long-term relationship. At some time during this journey we may want to get married, to announce before God and the world we have found our perfect match. <u>Just maybe.</u> My behavior sets the standard for my children to emulate, and I want them to be happy, unafraid of commitment

I can take care of myself having learned how to make and manage money, but probably can't afford to support my man, so if you're not financially secure, keep looking, because my real riches are a gift of the spirit. If you've never made a relationship last longer than a few years it's doubtful we would be a good fit. If I have to drive over an hour to get together with you and my dog's not welcome it could become cumbersome in a very short time. I am deathly afraid of motorcycles so please don't suggest riding off into the sunset together on one.

This thinking plays havoc with the heart. It doesn't fit into any of these boxes or choices provided. I am asking for everything and all this site has to offer, and all at once. It may take a lifetime for me to really get to know you; or, we may not progress beyond the first date. Do you think we can make a miracle happen?

Is there anyone left out there?

I'd really like to find a date for a concert this weekend.

I clicked on *Update Profile* and felt I had done a good enough job addressing the concerns Ben raised. Marriage was definitely a possibility but it wasn't exactly what I thought I wanted right now. I also was satisfied that I addressed those prospects who seemed to think because I was a lawyer I had more money than I did. I had enough to live on because of a lifetime of saving. I also wanted to eliminate those men who lived so far away that I'd have to hire dog care for our date. That was all I could do for the day.

When two quiet days went by without any responses, I signed back into the *Edit profile* feature and quickly changed my intent back to "looking for a relationship." I also edited a bit of the description to reflect that I wanted to begin with dating and see where that led. I didn't need to take a survey to know that just stating the intention of marriage was putting men off. I did a quick search online, to see how many local women were indicating that marriage was their intent. Only one young woman in her 30s showed up. I had only seen one or two men stating that it was their intention to find someone to marry and it hadn't seemed appealing to me either, perhaps just too serious for people who hadn't met or dated yet. When I had taken a quick survey of the morning coffee islanders, none of the dozen women thought marriage should be the stated intent—and they were all married women! Married people were under the mistaken impression that single people were having fun trying to find a date, and it was fun going out on dates with relative strangers. Actually, I was finding that searching online for possible dates was fun, but the dates themselves were fraught with uncertainty and apprehension.

I also deleted the entire paragraph pertaining to my requirements for a date since it didn't seem to flow with the rest of the text. However, I did think it was important, and thought it should be stated that if a man hadn't formed lasting relationships (over 10 years), rode a motorcycle, was not self-sufficient, lived more than an hour away and didn't like dogs, there was no point in contacting me. I was easily weeding out the men based on that criteria and it would be easier if they knew that before they tried to contact me. As it was, when such men did send a message, I just ignored it, which was inconsiderate. Men usually didn't try more than once, excepting for an apparent gigolo who kept flirting with me even though I told him I didn't think we'd make a good match, mostly based on his lack of a relationship that had lasted longer than four years.

Then suddenly there was a new message in my mailbox from Haiku4U which I eagerly opened.

You have such a wholesome face and optimism! It must be because you were with the 'right' one the first time. It looks like you just stepped off the Mayflower.

> *brown hair lengthens*
>
> *stroke after stroke*
>
> *sunlit swim*

Aren't we complex creatures?

Eliot

I wasn't sure what to make of his message. No one had ever compared my looks to someone stepping off of the Mayflower. From everything I had read about that tortuous journey people emerged weather beaten, half dead, and half of them in fact died the following winter. I couldn't figure why he had inserted a bit of poetry in the middle of his message. It was interesting, but a complete *non sequitur*. Still, it was a response and I was eager to line up a date for the upcoming weekend!

I left for the gym and contemplated how I should respond. Eliot hadn't exactly said anything about the weekend date I wanted. He hadn't really said anything at all in a cryptically poetic way. I considered just proceeding with a very straightforward approach and getting the weekend date squared away. I had vowed to the islanders I'd find someone for the upcoming Saturday night concert.

After my swim and shower following my daily gym routine, I sat back down to address Eliot. Before I did that though I saw there was not one, not two, but three more responses to my specific request for a date that weekend. Wow! What a difference there was in not putting the issue of marriage up front. I couldn't write back to Eliot and invite him over before examining the other choices. All four profiles of the respondents were checked out:

1. Stephen appeared in my Top 10 Prospects list:

    65-years-old, 5'10", Christian from Venice

    Business consultant, bachelor's degree

    Divorced, Actively seeking a relationship

    a maker (?)

    Wanting "a life devoid of materialism"

2. Haiku4u, aka Eliot

    63-years-old, 5'9", nonreligious from Bradenton

    Semi-retired, masters degree

    Divorced, relationship over 10 years

    Looking for a long term relationship

    Loves to write, trades stocks, white chocolate

    Would be content to make a new friend

3. Peaceman

    69-year-old, 6'4", nonreligious from St. Pete's Beach

    CEO of computer game business, some college

    Divorced from a long term relationship over 10 years

    Looking for a long term relationship with a nonreligious person

Lives on canal and would expect his woman to relocate

4. Tall & Handsome Gent

    51-years-old, 6'5", nonreligious

    Self-employed with some college

    Divorced with no relationship over five years

    Pictured in Scottish Highlands, Paris and London

Now that my mailbox was overflowing I noticed an emerging pattern: despite all the wonderful responses I received I was starting to find fault with all of them. I studied each entry with the most critical eye and seemed intent on finding that trait that made the prospect unacceptable. For someone who, just a week or so ago, was crying of loneliness this was totally inexplicable.

Stephen offered upfront to be my weekend date, but was too far away and used the expression "LOL" too often. I didn't know what that meant but didn't like the sound of it. Was it "lots of love", "lots of laughs", "laugh out loud", or "love to laugh"? Why did people use these stupid abbreviations? Was everyone working on a smartphone? He emphasized he was not into material things—did that mean he wouldn't be taking me out to dinner or buying me any gifts, like Ben? He had gone to the trouble to write two long notes, and he said he agreed with my sentiments entirely. It had to be the nasty picture of himself that turned me off most, posted and captioned with "Look at this Distinguished Man". He looked creepy.

I quickly eliminated him from the possibilities, mostly based on his photograph, and wrote back:

Dear Stephen,

Thank you for your lovely note. I tried to adjust my settings to reflect that I'm looking for someone within 25 miles of my home since I have trouble with sciatica when driving, and leaving my dog for more than just a few hours presents a problem. It wouldn't be fair to expect you to do all of the driving all of the time.

I'll have to pass on your offer to be my date, but appreciated your delightful response.

Anyway, your note made my morning feel so good and I wish you all the best of luck on this journey of love. Good luck finding that special one meant just for you.

Truly,

Katie

I hoped he'd get the message that I didn't want to pursue him, but no, within a few minutes he responded:

Katie,

I'm in the process of selling my house and am interested in relocating to your area. What spots would you recommend?

I couldn't deal with his request because I was too intent on lining up a date for myself without delay. I certainly wasn't going to suggest he move anywhere nearby me. He'd find a good place on his own. I ignored his message and moved onto my next possible weekend date.

This was not the first time I had heard from the Tall, Handsome Gent. His was one of those profiles that I had found disturbing for various reasons, the most notable of which was his lack of any real long term relationship when that was what he was purporting to seek. He was very handsome, and dressed in a dapper way that suggested that money was no object, but didn't hint at a career, which many of the successful profiles disclosed. He looked like a gigolo, and his multiple flirts he'd sent my way without text of any kind did not impress me. He certainly could be eliminated, and hopefully once and for all.

I wrote:

Dear Handsome Gentleman,

The age difference between us would make me feel like I was robbing the cradle. With your stunning good looks you'll have no trouble finding your special one on this journey of love.

Best of luck,

Katie

I got a text back almost immediately:

Your settings say your age range is from 50 -70

He obviously had a smart phone with instant messaging capabilities.

I went back to my settings and reset them to reflect I was looking for a man between the ages of 55 -70. No further response was warranted.

I was down to Haiku4U and Peaceman. Peaceman sported long ragged gray hair, which I considered very unsightly, and which he mentioned in his post by saying, "I'm not cutting my hair." Obviously other women had commented on his hair as well. I decided to ignore him for now especially since he was over an hour's drive away, focusing on Eliot, even though I was a bit perplexed by his message.

Dear Eliot,

When can we meet? I'm at the gym most mornings playing pickleball, but find most afternoons free. It's been too hot for coffee in the afternoon, but we may catch a cool breeze. What do you think?

I didn't want to waste anymore time with emailing when it really came down to whether he wanted to get together. A couple of hours later, I had a response from him:

Just recently, I had mild back surgery, so I will need some time to recuperate. I once was a tennis pro, so I'm having a hard time. Geez, look at all the attachments I have. Hasn't the weather been shockingly cool for Florida? Up until recently I was at the Y everyday. Now I'm a dermatologist's dream, depending on the equation, but I can't be in the sun. I always had to wear zinc oxide as a kid. Back when life was forever. I like intelligent women and romanticism—transitory moments. Give me time and I will meet you. Love to tinker with words:

> *Worn trail*

> *Beer bottles fill*

> *A red wagon*

A nickel, then, was money.

Till later,

Eliot

Wow, I couldn't believe how all over the place was his message. It sounded like his mind was racing and he couldn't quite catch up and capture the words to print. Why, if he were a tennis pro, would that make recuperating from surgery more difficult? I remembered he said he enjoyed writing but would have thought there would be more coherency to his note. His news that he was incapacitated set me back and I wondered if I were too hasty rejecting others who had stepped up to the bat in my time of need. This needed to be clarified right away.

Dear Eliot,

Your poetic endeavors are very reminiscent of William Carlos Williams and his famous red wheelbarrow poem, who was always one of my favorite poets, maybe because of the brevity used to evoke striking imagery.

I'm sorry to hear about your back surgery. I've never heard of any back surgery to be mild. A Canadian friend had something done last year to 'unfuse' the vertebrae but he didn't follow the doctor's orders and as a result the surgery failed. He was very sorry indeed that he hadn't taken all of the precautions as advised, especially since the nationalized Canadian health system would not permit a repeat surgery. So beware, follow your doctor's orders, and take care.

It comes as no surprise that you must protect your skin—you say in your profile you are red-headed and blue-eyed. One of my children has that combination too and she, like me, can't tolerate more than 10 minutes of being out in the sun. For years, just after I wash my face in the morning, I apply sun block and try to be generous. Now there are formulations with 100 spf, but anything with zinc is supposed to be the best.

Do you think you can be my date for the Saturday night concert here on the island? The Air Force Jazz Band will be entertaining the public at 7 p.m. at our Community Center, where you will find me working out most days. I was volunteered to help out at intermission selling snacks for a few minutes, but otherwise will be in the audience. It would be nice to have you. Let me know as soon as practicable.

I enjoyed your response and look forward to hearing from you again.

Until then,

Katie

Within the hour Eliot sent his response. Since it was almost 10 p.m. I took note that he must be a bit of a night owl. Even though I was already in bed I clicked onto his message

Hello Katie,

E.E. Cummings is one of my favorites, from love sonnets to poems of innocence. I have been published. Google me. Another form of poem has 5 lines and its barrels of fun writing. He was a real influence on my verse as was my grandfather who taught English.

> *Bells chime!*

> *A cactus rose*

> *grows from a sandbox*

> *where we first held hands.*

Actually my surgery wasn't that intrusive. The doctor burned the nerve. I've been in pain for two months since. It wasn't even called surgery; but pain management, which is a complete misnomer. There's 'street value' to the pills I have, says the doc. It's up to me to wean myself off of them. Since I don't have to work I trade options and write. My interests are varied—a real dichotomy. I'm not experiencing as much pain. I am a good patient, he is so good he is booked solid.

My parents were fair. I had a mouth like Cassis Clay when I played tennis, a real diehard, every day under the bloated tropical sun with no mercy. What fun.

The healing was exacerbated by going to the Y. Is 'free insurance' really free, in retrospect.

Why don't you call me: 941-362-0727

Here's from memory, written for another girlfriend:

A child

In her face

Gray strands

In whiter hair

At sixty-two

You gotta be kidding I get rich writing!

Oh, I'm allergic to, smiling, sun screen.

Eliot

Again, I was struck by the different directions Eliot went in his communications. He obviously enjoyed his writing and I was surprised with how many notes had passed between us that day alone (5). I found his writing vibrant and the more I read of his haiku poetry the more I enjoyed it. I noted that he incorrectly used the word "exacerbated," when I was sure he meant just the opposite. His use of fragments was also jarring, failing to tie together the disparate thoughts, using commas instead of semi-colons, but apparently the influence of haiku invaded all of his writing. I wasn't impressed and considered it tacky that he sent me poetry he had written for another woman. I went to bed feeling confident though that things were progressing well between us, even if he still hadn't addressed the weekend date invitation.

I waited until 10 a.m. the next morning before placing a call to him. It was time to progress to the next level of communication, especially considering his enthusiasm when it came to corresponding. Talking on the telephone was more personal for many people; but I preferred to correspond in writing and believed I read a person's true nature more accurately from the written word.

"Good morning, is this Eliot?" I asked when a somewhat groggy voice answered the telephone.

"Yes, sorry, but I'm just getting up. Still in a demi-dream state here. I was in so much pain last night I had to take a pain pill and it knocked me out," he responded.

"Oh, you did mention the recent back surgery. How long ago was it?" I asked.

"It's been two months and the doctor said it would take this long to recover. I had 15 years of pain prior to this procedure, which was a radio frequency therapy that heated the nerve. I told him about a movie during the surgery. Katie, how's your tooth?"

"Why do you ask?" There was nothing wrong with my tooth.

"You said you had to go to the dentist."

"You must have me confused with someone else," I said. "I'm the woman you were corresponding with on *POF* yesterday."

"You're right. I am confused and have you confused with a client of mine named Katie."

"What kind of business do you have?"

"I sell insurance products. It's a business I created for myself and provides a steady income from commissions. Best of all, I rarely work more than eight hours a month."

He made supporting himself seem relatively easy and I wondered how lucrative such a business was.

"Tell me more about yourself," I asked.

"I married young but it was a big mistake. My parents recommended I not get her pregnant and file for divorce immediately. I was with another woman for over a decade, but we never married because it would have ended the alimony she was receiving from her wealthy financier ex. She committed suicide when she was diagnosed with a rare degenerative disease which she knew would have required institutionalization."

I sat in shocked silence. This was the second man who discussed suicide as a viable option to living with a chronic progressive disease and it upset me. I remembered when Ben told me about his deceased friend who popped a lethal dose of sleeping pills when faced with a bleak diagnosis. He said it in an accepting way as though he were putting a stamp of approval on it. "He wasn't hurting anyone," Ben had said. "But we didn't ask to be born and I don't want to be the one to decide on death. How many people did he leave behind who may have been traumatized by his actions?" I had responded.

With Eliot I didn't respond at all, thinking about how much emotional trauma would be incident to having lived with someone who took her own life because of fear of the future. Shouldn't a life partner be there to guide the other through those tough times? I believed I had made my dying husband's days much more bearable by my support and presence. I felt a certain grace for having given the relationship its lifetime. Death was inevitable, but was it our decision to determine the exact exit date?

"Let me call you again around 7'ish," Eliot suggested in a rather preppy way.

"Good. Talk later then," I said, without disclosing how disturbing I found the conversation to be.

The call ended but my thinking about what he had said wasn't easily forgotten. Eliot seemed to be much more focused when he was talking on the phone, and I could forgive his confusion considering that he readily admitted to be under the influence of drugs. I hadn't asked exactly what drugs he was taking, but his reference to "street value" would put them in the opiate class. That he was so upfront about weaning himself off of them was consoling.

Promptly at 7 p.m. the telephone rang. I was very pleased to find him so reliable. The conversation revolved around his level of pain throughout the day. He was very happy that he hadn't had to use any pain killers during the day and even made it outside of his place for a short time. He was fairly confident he would be able to make it for the weekend festivities. I found myself listening more than talking, but the conversation moved easily and I felt comfortable.

The next morning I received a message from him via *POF*.

Hello Katie,

Hope your week is progressing nicely. I will call you tomorrow to plan another evening out. I love foreign films and just watched 'The French Minister' which isn't my typical favored romance but a political comedy that is vastly entertaining and I highly recommend it. Do you have Netflix streaming? Great escape without clichés. We can talk more.

> *Father grabs my hand*
>
> *in hospice*
>
> *barely breathing*
>
> *slowly beating*
>
> *heart.*

Till later,

Eliot

I found his poetry truly moving, and was touched by the image of the dying man. However, that he tended to insert his poetry within his messages to me still struck me as jarring and incongruous.

I responded to his message by calling him back. The hours were being whiled away and the phone calls went back and forth like a birdie lazily floating across the badminton net. The next day there were three calls of very long duration, and two the following, mainly to confirm the weekend plans, and decide where and when to meet. I was still reticent to invite strangers into the house even though we'd spend most of the week communicating with each other, one way or another. We were still strangers.

Eliot's pain steadily subsided throughout the week, and I thought the romantic interest was a powerful healing force. By Thursday Eliot had committed to being my date for both Friday and Saturday night. The local coffee shop was hosting an evening of one-act plays with food and, knowing many of my friends would be there, suggested that as well. There was a $20 fee, which I mentioned to him without any particular concern.

Just hours before we were to meet, I received a message from him. It seemed strange he continued to go through *POF* to contact me when we'd been conversing on the phone, but then I remembered I hadn't provided him with my email address. He captioned his message 'History v. Biography' and talked about Alexander Hamilton's duel with Aaron Burr and mentioned Hamilton's widow lived to be 97. "I can be Mr. Stoic, but not now," he remarked. Again, I was struck by the oddity of the information contained in the message. Was he just reading the biography of Hamilton and wanted to share it with me? Why did he label it 'History v. Biography' when historical biographies weren't adversaries? Maybe I just made too much out of every punctuation mark. Maybe he just wanted to share what he was currently reading.

Then, at the end of the message he again favored me with a poem which he said he had previously written. In fact, all of the poetry he shared with me had been written in earlier times with other people in mind, unlike the rhymes I had sent to Hugh which were inspired by our blossoming friendship. But his was good stuff, and I was enjoying reading it, even if I hadn't been the inspiration for it.

stormy night

ripe apples

drop from a tree

moonless night

undocumented aliens

gather rotting fruit

off the soaked ground

Can't wait to meet you!

Again, I was struck by how he inserted personal text into the message which was primarily a book review on Alexander Hamilton, and another sample of his poetry. He certainly wrote with a creative flair and corresponded eagerly and often!

Just before I was about to leave the house to meet him at the coffee shop another message sounded with a ping on the iPad. It seemed as if he were flooding me with messages. I clicked onto the site and found another note followed by a poem. He didn't even bother with any salutation.

Traditional poetry is always okay too, with a thimble of theology. This was written 20 years ago, most of my friends are Jewish, steeped in tradition. In church it's like being on the football field rather than watching it on TV. What do you think of the new Catholic bishop? Have a great day!

FIDDLER MOON

fiddler moon

with cracked toes

kicking the darkened sands

the peppered sky

now howling

incessant rage

P.S. Shopping at the Fresh Market sampling dish I gave at try a wonderful thing for two and so easy to make! A philosophy major, how delightful! Searching for the experience, total fruition and the answers.

Eliot certainly gave the impression of brimming over with enthusiasm and unleashed vitality. There was no more mention of his back pain. That's how pain was: it completely dominated when present, and was totally forgotten when it subsided.

Unbelievable as it was, Eliot managed to squeeze in one more message before I left the house. It was entitled "lemons" and stated, " adding lemon juice could reduce high blood pressure as well as cure urinary tract infections." Who cared? He had said he had high blood pressure so maybe a natural remedy was very important to him.

I finally, after what seemed like infinite interruptions, was ready to leave the house to walk to the coffee shop where we were to meet. The shop was hosting the Odyssey Theater and I had reserved two tickets, but hadn't paid for them. I had to stop at the ATM to get enough cash to pay for myself, just in case he didn't offer to pay for them both. I had no intention of paying for Eliot, and wondered if he would offer to pay. He had said he would take me out to eat the following night. I wasn't counting on his paying.

I kept mental picture of how he described himself in his profile and shown in his picture: 5'9", athletic build, red hair, blue eyes. He had gone out and bought himself a new outfit at Macy's earlier in the day. He bragged he had gotten a Nautica shirt for $29, regularly priced at $90, with assistance of coupons. Along with that he had bought himself matching yellow trousers. During one of our earlier communications I had suggested that since it was 95 degrees outside and we were attending an outdoor event that he might prefer to wear shorts and sandals. He could save the new outfit for our second date, the following night, which would be inside the air conditioned Community Center.

Another call from him was received around 5 p.m. "I'm leaving now."

"Good. If you take the coastal route it should take about an hour," I said.

He called again at 6 p.m. "I'm at Haley's Motel. Have I gone too far?"

"No, you're just about five minutes away. I'm leaving the house too; I'm just ten minutes away."

We hung up. I took one last look in the mirror and applied another squirt of perfume. I didn't want to arrive smelling like Benjamin. Off I went, wondering what would lay in store for the evening.

As I approached the coffee shop I spotted him sitting on a chair on the veranda. He resembled his photo. However, at age 65 he didn't have a strand of red hair left on his balding head.

"Hi, Eliot," I called out gaily, waving at him as I approached.

He stood up to greet me. If he were 5'9" then so was I, but I knew, especially since I just had a physical, I was 5'6". He had a bit of a hump protruding from his slouched posture. He exuded nervousness and had a slight twitch to his right eye. I did not find him at all attractive or appealing, contrary to the impression I had from the long, friendly telephone conversations. He gave me a peck of a kiss on the cheek then sat back down on the Adirondack chair. He sat a bit hunched over while leaning forward. I took the chair next to his, but unlike his, was receiving full sun. Already my body was covered in a glistening sweat from the short walk through the Bayfront Park.

"Would you like this?" he asked as he tendered a bottle of water.

"Yes, thanks, but you know drinks are included with the meal tonight," I said while wiping the sweat from my brow and taking a gulp of the lukewarm water.

"I recycle the bottles—just refill them for reuse," Eliot volunteered.

Ugh, I thought. It had appeared the seal on the bottle's cap had been broken when I opened it. I doubted that he washed the bottles in between refills—why waste the water?

"I do that too with my water bottles for the gym," I acknowledged as I recapped the bottle and handed it back to him. I had no desire for anymore of his recycled water. I certainly would have never offered anyone one of my used bottles.

"Have you checked in yet?" I asked.

"No," he replied looking somewhat dumbfounded. I had told him I would make the required reservations for two and what the cost would be.

"Let's check in then" I suggested while standing. He followed me through the beaded curtain door into the coolness of the shop, which thankfully felt 20 degrees cooler. We approached the desk, walking in a single file through the narrow aisle. I was ahead of him.

"I made reservations for two under the name Katie," I told the clerk.

"It's $20 per person and includes the show, wine and dinner," the clerk reminded us.

I quickly turned and looked at Eliot. He seemed not to be registering what was going on, but silently stood behind me.

"I'll pay for one," I said, taking out my wallet and removing a $20 dollar bill, which I placed on the counter. He made no offer to pay.

There was another strike against him—and within the first five minutes! First he had no red hair, he was shorter than he said he was, then he gave me used water!

Things weren't going so well. I moved aside so he could take care of his own dinner tab. He must not have remembered that in my *profile* I listed "being wined and dined" as one of my *interests*.

We moved further inside to admire and taste the expansive spread of appetizers—all organic and all healthy: types of hummus, tapenade, guacamole, olives and a tray of cheeses to be tasted on small brown paper places made from recycled materials. It was not only politically correct, but also good tasting.

There was a wine table set up with a dozen types of wine to choose from and the fellow serving went to great lengths to describe the nuances of each wine. He poured me a glass of Italian red, using an aerator to give full body to the taste. It was very impressive.

Together we moved outside, but all the shady spots were taken on the porch. There was no cooling breeze to deflect the intensity of the late afternoon sun that bore down.

The ten minute play was just that: two alcoholics who were involved in a fatal crash due to intoxication, meeting in hell where an open bottle of vodka they could not touch sat in between them. They fell in love but when they tried to touch electrical shocks forced them apart.

It was obvious the author had first hand experience with either living with, or being, an alcoholic. Hiding bottles around the house, sneaking drinks wherever and whenever, lying about drinking to oneself and others, was all explored. It was surprising how good it was, except for the relentless sun beating down on the audience, which had the effect creating the feeling that one was in hell along with the two characters in the play.

All the activity excused us from talking much to each other. After the play dinner was served. My friends from coffee—eight of them—were in attendance and Eliot was introduced to them all. He seemed to hold his own in exchanging everyday pleasantries, but made a bit of a faux pas when he described how he got out of active service in Vietnam while speaking to an army surgeon who had served there for years.

Eliot didn't eat much. When dessert was served, he skipped it altogether, claiming, "I don't have a sweet tooth." I took an extra chocolate strawberry and cannoli on his behalf.

It seemed his slightly nervous twitch had subsided. There had been a slight trembling to his hand, which persisted and became more noticeable when the hummus slid off of his plate and onto the floor. As the affair was winding down, the evening air was finally bringing relief from the heat.

"Let's walk over to the Gulf for the sunset," I suggested. We took off down the street and once on the beach plopped down to watch the sun disappear from the sky. I was finding Eliot easy enough to be with, but there was something about him that was odd, that didn't show up on written correspondence or through our long chatty phone calls. Once the sun set we strolled back.

"Let me show you the historical buildings and canal front garden before you go," I suggested. We stepped into the darkness of the jungle-like garden when my cell phone rang.

"It's my son, excuse me while I take it," I excused myself.

"I have to urinate," declared Eliot. I turned away, hoping my son who was calling in hadn't overheard his remark.

Suddenly I heard some children screeching, "That man is pissing in the bushes!"

"I have to go," I told my son while hanging up the phone, hoping he hadn't overheard the children's remark.

Eliot emerged from behind a bush. "They didn't see anything," he declared. Without much more conversation we walked over to his parked car.

I refused to shake his hand goodbye. Was that the reason behind the "lemons" communication? Did he have a urinary tract infection? I couldn't get away from him fast enough and wished I hadn't booked him for the concert the next night.

On Saturday I called Eliot to confirm we were still on for the evening even though I had already begun searching for new dates online.

Eliot said, "I made some fish stew three days ago. Can I bring it over for dinner? Otherwise, I will have to throw it out."

"Okay," I agreed half-heartedly. Evidently the dinner out he had promised me was off. I really didn't want him to know where I lived or inside my house even though he seemed harmless in a quietly passive way.

He arrived timely but had trouble finding the house, having turned the wrong direction on Bay Blvd. I went outside and stood at the end of the driveway, giving him directions on the cell phone. Obviously his rental car did not come with navigation. He was wearing his new outfit from Macys, and I noticed that the shirt was a bit too snug around the middle. The middle button looked like it could pop. When Trooper ran up to greet him, Eliot seemed taken aback, which was not a good sign.

He arrived with his pot of fish stew which he held above his head while entering the house and away from the dog. He was shown to the dining table. I served it into two soup bowls and didn't wash out his pot afterwards because there was a bit of stew left and I was sure he wouldn't want to throw it out.

We left for the concert at the Community Center.

"Why don't we ride bicycles?" I suggested.

Eliot had said he ended up making his living from being a tennis professional, which hinted to me that he must be in top notch shape. He had graduated with a creative writing degree (that explained his free spirited use of vocabulary) but when he couldn't get a job he went back to teaching tennis, for which he could earn $20 per hour.

I took the lead on the bikes and led the way alongside the park. We crossed over the small bridge spanning a canal and then onto the boardwalk adjacent to the pier. Just as we were getting there I heard a bit of a crashing sound. I turned my head in time to see Eliot rolling out from under an overturned bike. His arm was bleeding on his brand new $29 Nautica shirt, and grease stained his newly purchased yellow slacks. He claimed to be okay, but the swatch of scratched and bloodied skin on his upper left arm appeared otherwise.

"If the bike didn't have flat tires I would have been okay," he declared.

I looked closely at the tires. They both looked fine to me. I said nothing, sensing his embarrassment but also noting that he was subtly claiming the accident was my fault, since I had allegedly provided a bike with defective tires. It was troubling to think he may have injured his back, after having just gotten over the pain from the surgical procedure.

My friends at the Center were certainly going to be impressed when they met him, bruised and bleeding. Upon entering the Center I pointed Eliot to the men's room so he could take care of himself.

I checked in with the staff since Eliot and I were slated to sell snacks during the intermission. When Eliot emerged from the men's room he held a bunch of wet brown paper towels against his arm. We entered the gym and found seats along the aisle so we would be ready to jump up and attend to snack sales.

It was a relief when the music started and we didn't have to make a pretense of talking. I felt humiliated for Eliot, but resented that he needed to blame the mishap on me.

Eliot stood in the background during the snack sales, and I felt as if I were attending to the hungry crowd alone. Since I knew lots of people there and greeted many of them, while Eliot knew no one, I imagined he must have felt a bit isolated. When we made our way back and took our seats, Eliot turned to me and asked:

"Do you know what really impressed me most about you?"

"No," I responded, anticipating a compliment would follow.

"You never had to go to the bathroom the entire time last night."

What could I say to that? It was a relief when the lights dimmed.

After the concert I very slowly led the way back and we arrived in the darkness without further mishap.

"Don't forget your pot," I yelled while entering the house, leaving Eliot outside alone to safely dismount from the bike.

I grabbed the pot off the stove top, returned outside and handed it to him.

He took hold of it and moved off towards his car. He glanced back toward me and looked like he was about to say something, then changed his mind, opened his car door and stashed the pot on the passenger seat.

"Wait," I said, grabbing the bottle of Shout and spraying it liberally on the grease stains. "Maybe this will help."

Eliot said nothing as he got into the car.

The look he gave me in parting could only be described as wounded. It appeared we were both relieved the date was finally over and we were both off the hook.

Sarasota Bill

It was becoming increasingly easier to progress from the initial contact on *POF* with a prospective date to an actual meeting. The choices included marking someone as a "favorite" then waiting to see if that evoked a response; marking someone as "someone I'd like to meet" and waiting to see if the respondent answered; pressing the "flirt" button, and again, waiting; or, sending a quick message.

Electing to send a message with a photograph attached was resulting in responses nearly 100% of the time and was definitely the way to go if you were actually intent on meeting someone and not just sending emails back and forth like distant pen pals who weren't quite ready to reveal themselves.

Another realization was setting in: someone could look good on paper, sound okay on the telephone, but still be a dud when met in person. It only took a few minutes in each other's company to discern whether there was any chemistry. Either you felt some bit of attraction, repulsion, or virtually neither, almost at first sight.

Sometimes it took a bit longer, maybe a kiss or two, along with a hug. With the diplomat the first greeting, a French styled kiss on the cheek, was overwhelming because of his body odor from sweating from his walk down the street in the intense heat and humidity of the Florida day.

It was a turn off, and I had recoiled, but it was understandable and I too probably had worked up a sweat from walking with the dog from the house to the Olive Oil Outpost almost one-half mile away.

With the poet I could not remember any discernible pheromonal reaction; if anything, the meeting was just blah. I could tell from the first glance though that there was something insipidly weak about him. It was something that just wasn't attractive. Something told me that date was not going to go anywhere and booking the second date in advance, to have the weekend full, a hasty mistake.

But they were history! The hundreds of men wanting to be met beckoned me back to the web, like a child rich with weekly allowance money entering a candy store. All of Eliot's talk of the puny funds he earned, the dollars he saved shopping at Macy*s with coupons, made him seem petty and small. Maybe if he'd ended up buying me a drink or dinner I may have felt differently. He was cheap, and cheap with me wasn't impressive.

I needed to set my sights higher. I went back to browse, concentrating on men the website claimed were my "matches," ultra match," or "prospects."

POF predicted that if people ended up with each other, it was most likely they would have come from these lists.

Computers were rarely wrong, right? That was a good enough place to start. The ultra matches numbered 70.

Again today Diamonds4u popped up as first on my list. I moved on, determined I was not going to run after Hugh after what I perceived was a rejection. I scrolled down the list. There he was again, number 33—Sarasota Bill: A Great Catch Just Looking to Get Caught. What kind of bait would be needed to catch him? I remembered on my first days on the site I had sent him a "flirt" which hadn't provoked any response. His profile was short, but looked interesting:

> 70-year-old, 6', Catholic seeking long-term relationship
>
> Graduate degree, consultant
>
> Divorced, having been married over ten years
>
> Interested in boating, golf, theatre, jazz and collecting cars
>
> Former president of Fortune 500 Company
>
> Seeking a woman of character

I had to pause to consider exactly what he meant by the last entry. My first thought was he wasn't looking for a bimbo, just another pretty face to take to bed. It was intriguing. Could he mean "a woman of character" in the biblical sense, a God fearing woman, a woman of high moral standards? Or was it something more in keeping with an interesting woman who was a success in her own right; someone who had accomplished great things, or maybe someone who didn't fool around? I also noted the affected spelling of "theatre", of English origin in usage from the 1500s, which evoked a rather strained cultured tone.

Mentally I began composing my note to him. What exactly would impress a man who had made his fortune, presumably while working as the president of a Fortune 500 company? Those executives were typically paid well; the *Times* reported CEOs of such companies often earned 400 times what any other regular employees made. Of course, maybe he worked during a time when those gargantuan salaries weren't the norm, or weren't awarded to presidents instead of CEOs. I imagined how charismatic such a man would have to be to achieve such success in his career.

I decided to just write and tell him about myself, what I had done, why I found him attractive, why I didn't think the age difference of 11 years mattered, and what interested me about him. The letter wrote itself.

Dear Sarasota Bill,

Your profile is still up and listed among my top prospects. It intrigues me because of its striking brevity, which demonstrates a considerable measure of self-confidence, and allows the imagination to fill in the blanks. You appear to be the most successful and distinguished man featured, and I always admired people who excelled in their careers. Your interests are of interest to me too, but, although my father took to the golf course whenever he was free to find his serenity, I have never taken up the game, having found it hard to hit the ball and make it go anywhere near where it was supposed to go.

There's much my profile doesn't say about me. I made a life with the same man for 34 years, mostly in New York on Long Island. It wasn't easy, but was satisfying, especially to hear him say just before his death that he always loved me and I was the best thing that ever happened to him in his life.

We married about two years after we met, raised two children and practiced law together for 30 years. It was a real "family" practice, sharing the office with my father-in-law and mother-in-law, who acted as our legal secretary, when they were alive and well.

On weekends we'd all get together again for Sunday dinner, and sometimes took weekend getaways to places like The Plaza, when it was still just a hotel, or Hershey for the kids. We worked hard, made a good life and enjoyed each other's company. We believed in providing the best education we could for our children, so most of our money went into that.

My children all have bachelor's degrees: my daughter attended Smith then transferred to William and Mary, and my son from Boston College in 2011. I consider this to be my greatest success, and hope my children are prepared to meet life's challenges.

I came from a family in which my parents raised six children. My oldest sister is 15 years older than me and we are the best of friends, as I am with my brother who is 11 years my senior.

My husband was born in 1944 and died in 2011. You and he would be the same age. After my husband died I had one boyfriend who was 13 years older, and it wasn't our ages that was the cause of our breakup almost 10 months ago. I have morning coffee with the islanders at 7 a.m. on Tuesdays and Thursdays, any our group ranges in ages from 60 (me) to 92.

I also play pickleball at the Community Center most weekday mornings, and the players also range in age typically from the 50s to low 80s. I point this out only to address the apparent age difference between you and me, and say that such differences in age never seemed to matter much in my relationships.

As a result of my upbringing, I find it very lonely and almost unnatural to live alone. Having been left the dog from the children is of questionable consolation. I am making a good life for myself on this friendly island, but want for the intimacy which has defined what I have become. I am still licensed to practice law in the State of New York (no felon on the loose here) but have no desire to return to that lifestyle, choosing instead a simpler and kinder existence. Sometimes, however, if someone needs to talk or wants some forms I will still try to be of service.

I would like to know more about you. It seems you have not fully embraced retirement so must still derive some satisfaction from working. Over which company did you preside? How do you rate this method of trying to find a mate in an increasingly electronic world? How do you define a "woman of character"?

If you would rather talk, give me a call at (941) 778-1212 and we can schedule a date in between fishing expeditions!

All the best in this endeavor,

Katie

I checked it over, waited a few hours, checked it over again, uploaded it to the website's messaging center and pressed the "send message" button. Done. The message was sent.

Within an hour I was making mental bets with myself over whether he would respond. As if an epiphany, I realized all the consideration over the 10-year age difference could have been completely misplaced. He may be looking for a woman 30 years younger! What a fool I was making of myself. I didn't care. I was 60 and either I went after what I wanted while I was still attractive and healthy or I was just letting my life go by, not living it, but watching it out of the window.

There was the benefit of the anonymity on the web; he, like me, could simply ignore the message and by his silence I would have gotten his answer. One thing I could do without upgrading to a monthly fee was to check to see if he had viewed me. He had. By evening I was convinced he was not going to be interested in me. He was out of my league. But then, since he may be in a class almost by himself, what other woman would qualify as worthy? There were plenty of wealthy women on Longboat Key. I wondered who his prospects and ultra matches were. More than half of mine didn't even have a college education. I wasn't going to worry about it. After all, there were plenty of fish out there!

I slept well and awoke without any expectations of any kind. I clicked on my iPad and voila, a new message was in on my email screen from

Sarasota Bill. I deliberately made my coffee, fed and let the dog out, and took my vitamins while waiting for the water to boil. Then I sat, my mind clear and ready for whatever the day might bring. I clicked onto my new message.

Hi Katie,

Thank you for the nice note (almost a brief)! It's very informative and you seem to be quite a lady. I'm out of the city until Tuesday afternoon and will call you Tuesday p.m. . . . many thanks for the telephone number. . . I look forward to talking with you. . . . thank you again for your interest and. . .

Be careful out there,

Bill

It felt warm and sincere. I had no doubt he would call Tuesday afternoon or evening. I waited a bit, then sent off my reply.

Dear Bill,

Why would a lawyer say something simple and true, like 'I'd like to meet you,'

When it could be said in 1,000 words and become utterly confusing, too?

I'm typically home in the evenings after sunset to enjoy the day's lull,

and am excited at the prospect of receiving your call.

In fact, I can't imagine a more excited state,

Unless you were to ask me out on a date!

After I wrote you I did have one fear—

You may have found me too old for your taste, my dear.

Thinking of you,

Katie

He wrote again in the evening and his note sounded upbeat and humorous.

Dear Katie,

I keep a 38 next to my bed. Actually, I wish you were older, 70ish would suit me fine.

Are you a bit of a poet?

Talk to you soon,

Bill

I didn't see any need to respond again. It struck me as odd that he hinted he wanted an older woman, but I figured it was just to assuage my doubt over our age difference. He said he would call the next evening and I felt certain he would. A successful man kept his word.

There was nothing else to do but wait, and formulate ideas of what to talk about for our first call. I reviewed his short profile and highlighted all of the things we had in common. There were the obvious and superficial similarities which probably didn't matter: both nonsmokers, living in Florida, Caucasian, having had relationships over ten years, blue eyes, not wanting children but having adult children over 18, semi-retired, both with cars.

Actually, having had long relationships was quite important, since men who hadn't lasted long with any woman set off a red flag. I thought it showed the inability to form long lasting relationships. Then I listed the similarities which were more important to me:

1.) graduate degrees;

2.) wanting a long term relationship;

3.) enjoying theater and traveling;

4.) liking jazz.

In anticipation of the call going well, I did a quick search for live jazz in the surrounding areas. Marina Jack's in Sarasota had a group called the Venturas every Wednesday from 6 – 10 p.m.; Don Cesar Lobby Bar in St. Pete's had a jazz quintet on Thursdays, Fridays and Saturdays from 8 – 12 a.m.; 15 South Restaurant in Sarasota offered a jazz jam on Mondays and two places in Siesta Key offered jazz entertainment on Sundays— Ophelia's on the Bay for brunch, and Blasé Café and Martini Bar in the evenings. Those were plenty of nearby choices.

Then, in case I got tongue-tied I wrote a list of questions I might ask him to get a conversation going, or move it along. I came up with topics I hoped any man would find enjoyable to talk about.

1.) Tell me about your typical day in your current state of semi-retirement.

2.) What does a president of a Fortune 500 company do?

3.) Tell me more about your children, interests, hobbies or pastimes.

4.) Tell me what you care passionately about.

5.) How are you finding the online dating experience?

Shortly after sunset the phone rang and caller ID showed that Wm E. Long was calling. I picked it up on the second ring and answered as calmly as I could with a simple "Hello."

"Hello, is this Katie?"

"Yes, is this Sarasota Bill?"

"It was very nice to receive your note. Most people don't have that much to say," he commented.

"I just felt like telling you about myself. Tell me more about you," I suggested.

"Well, my father died when I was just a boy. He was a lifelong smoker, sometimes smoking over two packs a day, and developed and died from lung cancer at age 44. My mother was challenged to raise three young boys, but managed, with the help of her family and the church, to go back to work and earn a living to support us. In those days it was rarer for women to be in the workforce. She was a very devout Catholic and continued working until her dying day even though she had no need to do so."

"Is she still alive?" I asked.

"No, she died when she was 74-years-old." Mentally I made a note that longevity was not on his side. Scott's parents had lived into their 100s and he just naturally assumed that he would too. I wondered if Bill worried that he was approaching the end of his life, but couldn't think of a tactful way of phrasing the question. No one knew the exact time or place.

"It must have been hard for you," was the only lame comment I could muster.

"Well I got all types of jobs early on—newspapers sales, delivery boy and then received a scholarship to college because of basketball. In my third year of college I suffered an injury and lost the scholarship. I got a job with the teamsters and was able to complete my studies at the local public university in Columbus, Ohio."

"That's horrible that your scholarship was revoked because of an accidental sports injury!" I exclaimed with a real indignity.

"That's the way it was then. It maybe different now," he said.

"What are doing in your semi-retirement?" I asked.

"When I retired I started my own consulting company and continue to keep active with that. I was always obsessed with making money. My marriage was a casualty of my career. My son is also involved in it and runs it mostly by himself, in Columbus."

I was dying to know more about the company job but again found myself tongue-tied. He was speaking easily in a confident and animated way, just as I supposed a very successful businessman would. People don't succeed in business without a lively personality and ability to converse easily with everyone they meet, and he was no exception.

I changed the subject to something more frivolous.

"How are you finding the online dating experience?" I asked, referring to the list of possible questions.

"I've had a few dates, but don't even check my profile but for every week or two."

I was reticent to tell him that I was spending hours everyday online, enjoying the search and weeding through hundreds of profiles.

"How about you?" he asked.

"Well, I just signed on ten days ago. I had resisted the online dating experience mainly because I knew of a couple who did get together online and it had turned out badly because the man was a bit of a liar. But I got tired of moping around the house and feeling sorry for myself and am having fun, having arranged five dates with three different men, none of whom will I be seeing again."

I added the last part in an attempt to assure him that I was not into dating multiple men at the same time.

"You know Bill, in anticipation of this call leading to a date I was looking at different venues where we might meet that offered live jazz entertainment. I like jazz too."

Bill chuckled a bit and asked, "Like where?"

"Marina Jack's in Sarasota says it has live jazz on Wednesdays," I suggested.

"Hmmm, I've been there," he said, not too enthusiastically.

"I have too and the entertainment is really like background music. There's Don Cesar's in St. Pete's that has live jazz on Thursdays through Saturdays," I continued.

I didn't feel it necessary to go any further in the list.

"That's nice," he agreed. "Why don't we just plan to meet for lunch tomorrow?" he asked.

"Well, tomorrow afternoon I regularly play mah jongg with the ladies," I said. There was no reason to appear too eager. "What about dinner?" I suggested boldly.

"I have a dinner engagement with a woman who thinks she wants to move to Naples who I have scheduled to meet. I have to talk her out of it," he countered.

"Perhaps we can get together this coming weekend," I said.

"Let me see if I can rearrange this dinner engagement. I can call you tomorrow," he said.

"Great Bill!" This was a good sign. He was already putting me at the top of his priority list. I could see that lightning was striking over the Bay. "Bill there's lightning and thunder. I think I should get off the phone."

"Goodnight then. I'll call tomorrow," he said as he ended the conversation.

Having been up talking gave me a renewed energy as engaging evening activities are prone to do. Since caller ID had listed his full name, which also matched what he had provided verbally, it was typed into a Google search to see what more could be learned about him.

The first item to pop up that seemed to match his exact name and general locations of residence he had mentioned showed something odd—this Bill was listed as 81-years-old, not the age 70 listed on his profile! The only other man with that exact name, and there were only a couple of possibilities in the U.S.A., was listed as 55, just a few years younger than me, and lived in Columbus.

That man must be his son. A sinking, sick feeling overwhelmed me. I didn't want to go out with a man and be mistaken for his daughter. I didn't want to enter into a relationship where I might be scorned by his family, and possibly even my own. People might think I was just after his presumed money, and although I admired a man who had made a fortune, it was not my primary motivation, having learned how to take care of myself adequately enough.

The next morning I polled the islanders at coffee to see what they thought of my dating someone 21 years my senior, and whether he should be excluded from further consideration on the basis of beginning a possible relationship with a lie. How many women lie about their ages? Lots. The consensus was that it shouldn't be a bar to a first date, since the initial meeting might be a disaster on other unrelated grounds.

Many couples with disparate ages were compared: a niece who was lovingly involved with someone 23 years her senior for over three years and quite happy; Jackie Kennedy with Aristotle Onassis (33 years between them) and everyone wanted her to be happy after all she suffered even though maybe she wasn't.

Harrison Ford was with a woman 22 years his junior whom he married in 2010; Lauren Bacall became the 4th Mrs. Humphrey Bogart which an age gap of 25 years and they loved and worked together until his death over ten years later; Clint Eastwood, known as a womanizer, was with someone 35 years his junior for over 16 years now; Celine Dion married in 1994 her manager 26 years her senior; Oona O'Neill married Charlie Chaplin with an age gap of 36 years and she was his fourth and final wife, staying together for 34 years; actress Susan Sarandon was reported to be with a man 36 years her junior. Such unions may represent less than 1% of the population when comparing similarity of ages in marriages, but they happened.

While musing over this new found obstacle to pursuing anything further with him, a call came in from Bill's car phone. It was a bit fuzzy, but he quickly asked, "Sarasota is a bit far for you, where would you like to meet for dinner that's more convenient?" He had cleared his schedule, just for me. He wanted to go out of his way to meet me and let me stay close to home. It was endearing.

"The Beach Bistro in Holmes Beach consistently gets good reviews. We can meet there for a drink first," I suggested. It was reviewed as one of the best restaurants in the State of Florida, and also one of the most expensive as well. After what I found out about him I didn't care about the cost.

"Alright, what time?"

"How about 7 p.m.?"

"Good. See you then." A date was a done deal, in less than one minute.

How to approach the topic of the age difference with Sarasota Bill was the next consideration. The best, brightest, resourceful, imaginative and perspicacious minds I knew had to be consulted for that, even if it required making an international call.

The advice was not disappointing: ". . . raise it with him as soon as you sit down at the Bistro. . . . something like. . . 'I have a confession, I'm actually years younger than I said, but I appreciate an older man.'" This line was practiced several times while getting dressed, or perhaps slightly undressed, for the date.

 All the rest of the day's activities began to feel like filling up the time until the meeting: my friends, in between games of mah jongg, suggested how to dress, Jane advised me a relationship with an older man shouldn't be ruled out before it had even begun; a nap was attempted in late afternoon, but sleep was elusive even though I still felt drained from the blood donation a few days earlier; the dog was taken for a three-mile run until he was sure to collapse for the night upon returning home.

Rain began just as it was time to depart for the restaurant. Pulling into the lot an extraordinarily elegant late model shiny white Mercedes Benz convertible was spotted in the parking lot, bearing a license plate with his very initials. He said he collected cars.

I hoped he didn't collect women, too. He had arrived before me. The valet took the car and I made my way into the restaurant. The entry led into a bar.

There sat two couples--one was the local architect who was said to have just broken up with his girlfriend-- and one man by himself, partly shaded in the dim light. I stood nervously trying to catch the man's eye but he seemed oblivious to my appearance and was engaged in sipping a drink. I walked by the bar and behind the patrons and looked into the dining area. There was no one there to greet me. I returned to the entry way.

The single man seemed to resemble the photo of Sarasota Bill but I couldn't be sure. If it were him why wasn't he looking at me? The cell phone was taken out and both of his numbers, which had just programmed in, were dialed. There was no sound of a cell phone ringing at the bar. The man at the bar looked over and I tried to smile his way. I left a quick message on his second line that I had arrived.

For a second I considered leaving. As I was speaking into my cell phone I noticed the man at the bar was looking at me. I approached the bar to order a drink for myself. I edged in next to the single man who finally looked at me and asked, "Katie"?

"Bill!" I leaned forward and kissed his cheek as he put his arm around my waist in a sort of welcoming hug.

"You are beautiful," were his first words.

"Thank you. I just left you a message by cell."

The bartender asked, "Would you like a drink?"

"Let's go into dinner," he suggested, bypassing the option of just having a drink at the bar before deciding to have dinner together. It was a good sign. He stood up and our eyes were practically on level with each other. After my physical examination I edited my profile to reduce my height from 5'7" to 5'6"; his profile listed his height at 6', but he couldn't have been taller than 5'8".

What were men thinking when they posted their particulars, a physical exam at age 18? People shrank as they aged. He stood behind me while the waiter showed us through the crowded dining room to the best table in the restaurant, a table for two in the corner with ceiling to floor windows on both sides, opening to the expansive view of the aquamarine waters of the Gulf of Mexico.

"I believe in making reservations," Bill said.

"You take the seat with the view of the Gulf," I insisted, "I see it everyday." We sat and the waiter put a napkin across my lap with a flourish. As it slid to the floor I immediately ducked to retrieve it. As I sat up his eyes were penetrating and seemed to focus somewhere on my bosom. It was a relief when the waiter approached to ask what I'd like to drink. "Red house wine," was the easiest answer.

I knew now was the time to broach the matter of his true age. He looked like he could still pass for about 70; but then again he could be 81. When he stood he appeared a bit stiff, but since he had walked behind me into the dining room I couldn't judge by his gait.

The words, which I had practiced until they flowed easily, stuck in my mind, a long distance from being uttered. My tongue loosened a bit with the wine, but the topic of his age still was beyond me.

He bantered familiarly with the waiter as we decided to try an appetizer to share prior to ordering dinner. Should it be "Duckshroom": "Hedgehog and maitake 'shrooms in a clear vegetable duckling broth kissed with truffle"? We agreed on "Cheeky" which was described as "Fresh grouper cheeks and throats the captain cut. Bistro carved from whole grouper. Delicately sautéed and kissed with lime butter. Served with a dollop of chefs mashed." Wonderful. The chef believed in kissing his edible creations.

"Order whatever you want since I just came into some money from a small wager," he suggested. It was a nice way to let me know he was expecting to pay the bill.

"Let's try the Cheeky." I ruled out the bouillabaisse that was listed at $78.00, and the bottles of wine priced over $400. Conversation stayed on a light note, and there was laughter imagining his joy when winning a wager based on whether a football team's score would be an odd or even number.

"You know, I may be considerably younger than you," I finally blurted out. I may have added, "but I appreciate an older man," but then again I may have only thought it. I thought I managed to get all the words out.

"You look like you could be 52, or up to 55," was his response. The retin-A cream and Botox was paying off.

I sat quietly waiting to hear what he would say next. "It was a big deal when I turned 70," he added. (But when was that, was it 11 years ago, I should have asked) but, again sat dumbfounded and uncertain.

He changed the subject and serenaded me with stories from his business, information about his successful children, details about how his last relationship ended. The woman chose to play bridge with her girlfriends instead of attending a black-tie benefit at the Y where he was being honored. That really was unforgivable, but was that all to the story? Hadn't I just turned down his first invitation to lunch because of playing mah jongg with the ladies?

He wanted to know the address where I had practiced law; obviously he had been trying to check me out online too. We admired the scrumptious plates being served to the neighboring tables.

He noticed that the couple next to them celebrating their 37th wedding anniversary said virtually nothing to each other the entire time.

He owned a home in Sapphire Gardens, but had had a penthouse on Longboat and was bidding on a home on Bird Key. It all sounded wonderfully enticing; I could almost imagine myself helping him with the move.

The appetizer was delicious. When it came to ordering and I couldn't decide on the lobster or shrimp, he ordered the shrimp so that I might try it too. How considerate was that?

The food did not disappoint, even if the shrimp tasted like they had been dowsed with barbecue sauce. I spent a long time deliberating over eating the marigold that adorned my plate. I finally nibbled on the flower, which was rather bland, then hoped I hadn't proven to him I was an idiot!

When it came to dessert he balked. "Why spend $12 for a piece of Key Lime pie when you can get a whole one at Publix for less than half that?"

"It's the experience that you're paying for, Bill. Remember, you can't take it with you," I added.

When the bill came I excused myself to go to the ladies room. I took my time admiring the attention to the decorative details of the small and intimate restaurant. When I returned to the table Bill sat gazing out over the darkened Gulf of Mexico beach, mesmerized by the lightning storm in the western sky. There it was, the lightning I was expecting when I met my man.

He rose to greet my return and we exited the now empty dining room. Bill walked behind me lightly resting his hand on my back as if he were guiding the way for me.

"Look at that," I said, pointing to the framed photos of notable diners which were annexed to the ceiling. Bill chuckled in appreciation. At the door we handed our claim tickets to the valet who went to fetch the cars in the pouring rain. As we stood waiting Bill leaned forward and kissed me on the lips. It felt nonthreatening and lighthearted. I looked into his eyes, and then kissed him on the lips. The valet pulled up with my car, approached me holding out an open umbrella and I sprinted with him towards the open car door. "He'll take care of you," I said, indicating that Bill had some tip money in his hand. I jumped into the car, closed the door before more of the pounding rain could enter, fastened my seat belt and drove off.

I had no sooner gotten home than the phone rang. Caller ID showed it was from Bill.

"I'm just checking to make sure you made it home safely," he said.

"Yes, I had no trouble navigating the five minute drive in the rain," I said while laughing.

"Be careful out there," he commanded.

"You drive carefully too," I said.

"It looks like the sheriff is giving me an escort off of the island. He's been following me for several miles now." We hung up.

I thought that the local sheriff probably never saw such a fancy car before and was just mesmerized by it. I got online and tried to look up the type of Mercedes Bill was driving. It looked like a model that retailed new in the hundreds of thousands of dollars. He may have spent more on his car than I had on my house.

The next evening he called just after sunset when I had told him I was most likely to be at home.

"Bill, the dinner at the Beach Bistro was just one of the best I've ever had!" I said. "Some reviews make it the best restaurant in Florida."

"Hmmm, really," he queried. "One of my wagers came in. Are you busy tomorrow night?" he asked.

"No, I'm free," I responded.

"Why don't you pick a place for dinner," he suggested.

"What if I said I wanted to go to a certain café in Paris?" I teased.

"My goal is to make you happy," he responded, not missing a beat. "Shall I pick you up around 7 p.m.?"

"Perfect," I said. I provided him with my address and general directions. Since he'd been on the island the night before and I was just down the road a few minutes he should have no problem. "Oh, and Bill, I did want to know what famous consultant you used to come up with your catchy headline 'Great Catch just looking to get Caught?'"

He laughed heartily and said, "I had to fly to New York and consult with the experts on Madison Avenue for that one!"

I was excited when the post office called the next day to say that a package from Neiman Marcus was in for me. Only on their small island would the United States Postal Service provide such intimate service. I jumped on my bicycle and raced to pick up the package. The form fitting dress I had ordered just days earlier was just what I had hoped; its royal blue pattern flattering my skin tones, its just above the knee length ideal for showing off my lean legs, and the way it hugged my body revealed that I still had interesting curves. I felt confident I looked my best, and chose to wear the lapis lazuli Italian necklace and oversized oval earrings set in gold that my husband had gotten me on the Ponte Vecchio to complement the outfit.

Promptly around 7 p.m. I noticed his extravagant Mercedes pass by in front of my house. The door bell rang shortly afterwards, but like a fool I ran to the front door and swung it open only to find no one there. I raced to the back door and found him standing patiently. He stepped inside the house. I looked over his head and noted that the garage looked cluttered with stuff and vowed to try to organize it better.

I threw my arms around Bill and gave him a warm hug. I stepped back and gave him a once over from head to foot. "My, my, don't you look elegant tonight!" I exclaimed.

Indeed, he was dressed impeccably, in a navy blue blazer with gold buttons, a silk handkerchief jutting jauntily from the breast pocket, a gold necklace discernible under his silk button down shirt, casual brown Italian loafers, and sporting a black watch with squiggly minute and hour hands unlike anything I had ever seen anyone wear. It resembled pieces by Daniel Roth—a semi-oval case and squiggly hands in a royal blue, a piece that would retail for who knows what obscene sum of money.

"You dressed so nicely for our date that I thought I should do the same," he said without embarrassment. I was glad the new dress came in time for this date, but did not disclose that it was brand new, remembering Eliot's new outfit and how little I was impressed by it, especially when he disclosed the price tag.

I showed him in and indicated he should sit on one of the two bar stools at the granite counter that separated the kitchen and dining area. I had put out a bowl of almonds and some pita chips with a sweet and sour mango spread.

"Would you like a drink?" I asked. I remembered he drank scotch at dinner at the Beach Bistro so I took the half empty bottle of scotch left behind by Scott which was in the cupboard and poured a bit over some ice in one of the glasses Scott had purchased just to go with his evening scotch. Bill took the glass and came around the counter to add water to it. I watched him silently as he moved back towards the stool, noticing a limp emanating from his right side. I refilled my water glass and sat next to him on the other bar stool.

"Did you have any trouble getting here—did you get a police escort again today?" I asked.

"I took the Bay Shore Gardens Parkway to El Conquistador Parkway and was here in 30 minutes," he said in a complimentary manner. That was the route I recommended he try as a short cut to Sarasota. I put some spread on a pita chip and handed it to him to try. He obligingly ate it. Trooper came up and sat down in between us, with drool dripping from his mouth.

"Do you feed him from the table?" Bill asked.

"I do share my food with him," I admitted. "I've probably ruined him." I didn't care. Half of my food was better off in Trooper's stomach. I talked about the renovations I had done to the house since I had purchased it. He mentioned a woman whose husband built her a new house and she spent all her time decorating it. When the house was finished the husband suddenly died.

To me, it didn't sound like the worst way to spend time, but it would have been an empty accomplishment if there were no one there to share it with.

"Shall we go?" Bill asked when he had finished his drink and the clock was striking eight. We walked out through the garage to his chariot. How I wished I had straightened up the junk in the garage before he came. He opened the passenger door for me and I lowered myself into the seat. When he got to his side he pushed a button that made the driver's seat go backward to give him ample room to slide down and in. For such an expensive car it wasn't exactly the easiest thing to get into.

"What a fancy car you have Bill!" I remarked as if I hadn't already noticed it in the parking lot on our first date. He didn't know that I had noticed it. "I did check at our local restaurant overlooking the Bay, but they were booked for tonight," I said.

"And that was the only thing you had to do today! Don't worry, there are plenty of places." Bill drove slowly off the island, adhering to the 25 or 35 mile per hour speed limit. We drove into Bradenton Beach and down Bridge Street. I recommended the Blue Marlin, an upscale trendy place Scott had liked, but when Bill couldn't find a parking space nearby he said he'd need something closer. He drove onto Longboat Key and without consulting me further pulled into a shopping center and in front of a lobster restaurant.

"Shall we," he commanded.

I climbed out of the car and waited until he did too. I slowed my steps considerably until I walked in pace with him. Finally, I decided to just ask,

"Bill, how did you develop a limp?"

"I was in an auto accident and broke my hip. I was the passenger in a car that was broadsided. I had surgery, but the doctor said I have bone on bone now." His walking looked laborious and painful.

"How long ago was that?" I asked.

"It was about a year and one-half ago," he replied.

"I don't know what the statute of limitations is in Florida exactly, but it sounds like you still have time to bring a claim for injuries," I commented.

"No, it doesn't matter," he said.

"But Bill, you have a permanent injury as a result of that accident. That's what auto insurance is for. A claim like that is worth at least $100,000.00," I exclaimed. Bill said nothing further, having already decided he was not going to do anything about it. I couldn't believe anyone could be that blasé, especially when he refused to order dessert the other night because the piece of pie cost more than an entire pie from the grocery store.

"Why don't you talk to that famous personal injury lawyer you said you do consulting for," I persisted. "He'll tell you." Since Bill said nothing, I shut up on the matter. People certainly could be strange.

The restaurant he chose had recently been redecorated and looked upscale and clean. We were shown to a table overlooking tropical gardens outside in the rear. Instead of taking the seat across the table from me, Bill chose to sit next to me. The waitress asked if we'd like drinks. Bill ordered another scotch and I, my daily 5-ounce glass of red wine. We sipped our drinks while looking over the menu.

"What do you recommend?" I asked.

"The swordfish is good," Bill suggested.

"Great. Would you please order for me Bill," I directed.

When the waitress returned Bill placed our identical orders. His hand found mine and he covered it with his. Today he had a band aid on over the top of his hand, which showed signs of being black and blue.

"What happened?" I asked, touching the band aid.

"Oh," he declared, without elaboration. I let it go. The food was delivered very quickly and we silently ate. He didn't seem to have the animation of the first date, but then perhaps neither did I. It felt comfortable with him though, with no pressing urge to fill the spaces between us with sound. We both finished all the food on our plates, perhaps again reflecting a childhood lesson of not wasting food, finishing what you were given. Again I had to deliberate whether or not to eat the flower the chef had put on the plate. Tonight it was an orchid whose petals tasted smooth.

"I noticed one of your interests is a kissing contest," Bill mentioned.

"We're going to have to try that," I promised. As the plates were removed from the table I noticed that the dining room had emptied and we were the only diners left. I glanced over at his fancy watch but couldn't discern the time from the squiggly lines. It was probably close to 10 p.m.

He remembered exactly how to return to the house. He got out of the car with me and we stood in the driveway.

"This is a night of a honey moon," Bill remarked. The reddish hue to the June moon was how the getaway for lovers got its name. We moved closer together and he kissed me. I responded by kissing him several times on his lips, cheeks, and lips again, before withdrawing. I was uncertain whether he was expecting to be invited in. I decided against it. It was only our second date, and even though I didn't know what protocol was, I didn't feel ready to explore him more physically that evening.

"It was a very nice dinner," I said before pulling away and leaving him standing there as I went into the house through the messy garage.

I called Bill the day after our second date, but got his answering machine. I left a message thanking him for a lovely evening and telling him to call me again if his wagers came through. I hoped afterwards he took it as the joke I intended it to be.

The next day I saw that his number had called the house just one-half an hour before I'd gotten in, but no message was left. I immediately called him back. Again I got his answering machine and wished him a happy Father's Day. I let him know I had wanted to bring him a picnic lunch but thought that he was a very busy man. I was disappointed that I missed his call. It was hard to believe he had gone out at 9 p.m. on Sunday night. I kept the cordless phone next to me on the bed, but he did not call back.

On Monday I rushed home after taking Trooper up to the point to watch the sunset since that was the time he seemed most likely to call. It was the time I had told him I was most likely home. I sat next to the phone deciding that I would not call him again, since I had placed two calls in a row to him. I hoped he would call. Just after 9 p.m. when I was giving up hope, the phone rang and caller ID showed it was him.

"Hello," I answered in a friendly voice.

"Hello my darling," his voice boomed out in a warm and welcoming way.

"What have you been up to these past few days?" I asked him.

"Well, just as I'd hoped, my children all called in for Father's Day and I had very nice conversations with all of them. My one son is sometimes late, but he knows what day it is since he has two kids of his own. I was in the Home Depot during the afternoon and ended up hauling home two large sacks of goods."

"Are you the type of man who likes to putter around the house?" I asked.

"There's always something that needs to be done. Someone before me painted the rooms a god awful color, applying the paint with what appeared to be a mop. All of the switch plates were painted over. For

.69 I can afford to replace them," he said. "There were also a bunch of burned out light bulbs that needed to be replaced."

"Can you still get incandescent bulbs?" I asked as if it were a matter of great importance. "I understand that they are being phased out—something to do with not being able to recycle them."

"It didn't look like there were any 100 watt bulbs," he agreed. "There were those spiral ones that I never much liked."

"They've gotten much better in the past few years. The problem with the delay in switching on seems to have been corrected," I noted. "Or, you can get the halogen and low voltage bulbs that are supposed to last forever but cost about $30 each," I remarked, as if my extensive knowledge of light bulbs was something that was really going to impress him. I was grasping at straws, maybe trying too hard to converse.

"Well I just got the old kind," he said.

"Even those are different depending on whether they are soft whites, cool whites or day light. The soft light is usually more flattering." The conversation was becoming totally absurd but I couldn't seem to stop myself from chattering. Who cared? I was glad to hear his resonant voice and have him talking to me.

"I had a villa that I used to rent out. I got a call from a woman who had just taken possession the week before. She said, 'You know, not all the bulbs are working in the bathroom.' The bathroom had a light fixture with twelve of those round bulbs. I told her, 'Go into the garage, look on the shelf over the washing machine and you will find a box marked light bulbs. If you need any further help call me again.' Thank goodness she did not call back. It was those types of calls from the tenants that gave me reason to sell the villa."

"I used to draft leases for landlords. It was always made clear on house lease that the tenant had primary responsibility for routine maintenance under a certain amount of money." I hoped I didn't sound like I was bragging. I did in fact do that type of work and always made sure landlords would not be bugged for every little thing that had to be done.

"Just when I decided to sell the villa my neighbor put theirs on the market, pricing it substantially less than mine. I spoke to my son and we agreed that my unit was better kept and worth more. It sold for what I asked."

"That's good," I remarked. "Are you still thinking of selling your house?"

"Maybe. I have new neighbors who have been working on their house for over a year. There was a port-o-potty out front that was a real eyesore. Last Sunday morning when I was reading the paper in bed a car drove by slowly, turned around, came back and stopped. A well dressed woman in a black dress hopped out of the car and used it. You know, there's always someone who sees what you are doing."

"One of the men I had a date with, let's just call him dater #3, got caught," I said. "We had gone to an Odyssey Theatre production for a 10 minute play, then walked over to the Gulf for the sunset. I wanted to show him the gardens around the historical society. When we were there my cell phone rang. It was my son who wanted a wake up call for the next morning when he was scheduled to take his Chartered Financial Analyst exam. My date announced he had to urinate. Suddenly I heard some children shouting, 'He's pissing in the bushes!' When he came back he said, 'Don't worry, they didn't see anything.' We parted company without shaking hands.

Bill laughed wholeheartedly. "When the grandkids are over and In the pool they've announced they have to go. I tell them to just go in the pool. My daughter thinks that's terrible."

"Well, the chlorine should clean that up," I said although I agreed with his daughter; I never wanted kids pissing in the pool.

"What's with people wanting salt water pools?" he asked.

"Salt water is easier on the skin and swimsuits," I answered. "My neighbors across the street had renovations going on for the past year too. I think because the builders knew it was just their vacation home they were in no rush to finish the job."

"That could be the reason," Bill agreed. "I also had to buy some wineglasses. I had found some for .50 at a garage sale but didn't have more than two that matched each other."

"What do you need more than two for anyway?" I asked.

"Right. I've plenty of other drink glasses. I used to take them home with me when I hadn't finished my drink. I'm a real cheapskate. Some habits you never grow out of. Growing up poor always stays with you."

"Well, it's not exactly grand larceny Bill; maybe petit."

"I don't need anymore now." Bill said.

"I used to have dozens of wine goblets," I said. "When I packed to move south I ended up giving most of them to the rectory priests, since they were always hosting fancy wine events. They hosted the funeral luncheon for me in the dining room. It was a lovely Italian styled villa built by a former wealthy priest. The dining room was paneled in oak on the walls and ceiling, and there were ceiling to floor French doors that led out to a wrap around veranda. I only needed to keep a few wine glasses for myself. In New York I used to have all of the parties since I had the biggest house. Now I can host a couple or two, which is just fine."

"I don't have much call for more than that either," he remarked.

"We sold a lot of stuff like that at our church rummage sale. I was assigned to collect money with Rose, a 94-year-old woman who was with a man she met after her husband died last year. He was a neighbor and his wife had died a few years earlier. He came over one day and they've been together since. When she went to confession she told the priest she was living in sin and the priest just laughed. She spent the entire time trying on and modeling clothes, putting together a new wardrobe for herself."

Bill laughed appreciatively. I hoped he had made the connection between Rose, with her new found love, and us.

"Right. Well. . . ." the conversation seemed to be drifting off.

"Bill, I really wanted to bring a picnic lunch sometime. Would you like that?" I asked.

"Yes I would," he replied.

"What's your schedule this week?" I asked.

"I'm going to lunch tomorrow and will drive a friend to Moffitt on Wednesday."

"Isn't Moffitt the cancer research center in Tampa?" I asked.

"Yes, it is. Do you see a dermatologist Katie?"

"I just chose a primary care doctor who had treated my mother. He removed some growths with nitrogen oxide. The excess compound exploded in the sink when he discarded it! He said they were benign, but when he billed my insurance company $475.00 for the 15 minute visit he called them precancerous lesions." I wasn't ready to disclose I consulted with a dermatologist for facial skin care. Let him just think I was aging well.

"I had some lesions removed by my dermatologist," he said. "You have to expect that here."

It sounded like, with the schedule he had announced, he was too busy to see me. I wondered if he was expecting me to invite him to dinner. I remembered how endearing it was when he rearranged his schedule the week before to see me for our first date. I did not press the matter.

"You'll have to find something to do Katie," he said.

I wasn't quite sure what he meant by that. Was he implying I had to get busy since he would no longer be calling on me? "I do tutoring during the school year and lots of volunteer work for the community," I said.

"That's good," he replied.

"An 80-year-old doctor I play pickleball with most days said I should have an affair. I said to him, 'It's not that easy.'" I really couldn't figure why I said that, and he said nothing in reply. "I'm sorry we don't have a meeting planned," was all I could think to add. Still, he said nothing more about seeing me again.

"Sleep well my dear," he said in parting.

"Good night Bill," I answered. I hung up the phone with a sinking feeling like that may have been our last call.

As the realization sunk in that he was merely returning the call I had placed without committing to any future meeting with, I began to quietly weep. The tears washed my face with sadness.

Dating may be exciting and fun, but it was also starting to feel like an empty exercise in futility. What was wrong with me? Why had I monopolized the conversation with silly inconsequential remarks? Why was I stalling out after the second date, which was now a fact with three different men. For all of my worry that Bill was too old for me and his limp would make it impossible for him to engage in many physical activities, he was the one dumping me. What were his concerns? He had told me he thought I was beautiful. Was it that I was too young for him and he felt embarrassed to be seen with me? Was I not rich enough or engaging in conversation? We'd had lots of laughs during the phone call. Did he think I was just after his money as I had surmised about men who contacted me and were considerably younger? When I first contacted him I thought he was only 10 years older. He didn't know how lame his competition was. I retired to bed, taking an over-the-counter sleep aid so that I might fall asleep fast and stay asleep a very long time.

Just as I had suspected, in the following days there were no more phone calls from Bill.

Tony Dylan

There was nothing to do--one door was closing; it was time to open a window and allow the Bay breeze to blow away the stillness. It was back to the drawing board. I began by sifting through the *POF* prospects and matches that I had ignored. Earlier on I had received a note from Tony Dylan. He wanted to meet me, which was followed by a fairly lengthy message that sounded interesting.

Tony Dylan: Mickey seeks Minnie

55-year-old, 5'8", agnostic

Free thinker wants a long term relationship

Dunedin, bachelor's degree, simi/retired (sic)

Single, does not drink, dog

Interests: spiritual development, sports, boating, science, camping

Initially he fit my narrowed down requirements: he was looking for something long term and had been involved in a prior long term relationship. The fact that he did not drink was a bit of a red flag, as I was starting to interpret that as someone who may have had a problem with alcohol and was on the wagon. I wanted to avoid anyone who had the semblance of a substance abuse issue.

It appeared that he had used his real name and that seemed up front and honest. I noted that some of his incidental interests were nothing that interested me, and the fact that he lived more than 50 miles away was another reason it had been easy to ignore him.

But he was showing signs of persistence, and his note was creative and engaging, responding to my revised profile.

Hello Katie,

Are you a philosopher? I too would like to feel young and in love again, but I am disheartened by the number of my friends, family and acquaintances becoming ill, some terminal. . .hard to find joy in these circumstances.

Too many people on this site are dreamers setting forth with shopping lists for their next partner as if an order could be placed on Amazon for just the right person! It's all in the numbers, to get lucky and find that karmic match you may have to weed through dozens and dozens of interviews.

Love doesn't happen like it does in the cinema, and I have always been surprised by the ones I have fallen for. Please read my profile if you can make it past my mug shots.

Tony Dylan

He had an unusual flair with his words, and seemed to be speaking directly to me. That he had been frustrated with the number of women he had been exposed to without success was very consoling. One of his photos showed a handsome man sporting a head of dark hair sitting at a piano, and another of him with a large dog on the beach, which appeared to be Daytona, since the car was also on the beach.

I reread his *Description* of himself and it was similarly casually engaging and chatty.

Cheers,

It takes a stretch of dreaming to become involved in electronic romance. We really shouldn't be looking for a clone. . .how about, like when we were young, just getting together to hang out, steering clear of the bullies. The gods will be gracing us if it turns into something more.

Let's plan to do some biking in the morning before it gets too hot, or later for sunset. (I have a loaner bike handy for you!) When we dance I promise not to splatter on the floor. I can eat without spilling my food on myself. Walking far is hard for me. I collect a small retirement income and have a license which, along with some piano playing, provides me with good income. I will sometimes have a bit of beer but don't like the calories from it. Am eager to sail my boat far and wide with that special someone willing to wade through the silly muck. . . stuck. . . until our last breaths. I'm outta here within the next year or two. Let's do something interesting or let me be your escort to some event with good food!

I try to keep my life simple with daily meditation and soothing music, movement and good diet. I try to improve my habits everyday, delving into the subconscious through the meditative state, learned from living with monks. I am always having fun performing my music—look for me in those finer restaurants and seaside resorts.

I like odd friends but keep traditional ones as well, believing we are all bound to a higher karma. I was a single parent and work for an insurance company writing damage reports. I'm into the creative as well as the crafts incident to performing technical work.

The U.S. has been thoroughly explored but for Alaska. I could be doing tours on my next adventure.

I believe the U.S. is ruled by corporations corrupted by their own agendas but creating a money trail to the White House. Spending is out of control and their only solution is to print more money to cover their extravagant lifestyles. What will our children do when the rich have plundered our reserves?

I dwell in the 'big picture' and am honest, sensitive, mild mannered, and I forget the bull and drama.

LET'S EXCHANGE SOME GYM CLOTHING AND SEE IF IT EMITS JUST THE RIGHT PHEROMONES!

I'd like a movie or a play for a first date, but somewhere quiet to talk works too.

I thought there was an overall excitement to his profile and something refreshing in its perspective. I decided to respond.

Hi Tony,

It was nice to receive your chatty note. Reading your profile left me with a few thoughts and questions. I agree with you that this site may be more about finding like-minded people to do things with. I'm enjoying the process of putting myself out there for inspection and wondering why, during so many months of feeling quite lonely, I resisted the idea of internet meetings. My opinion was formed somewhat by having known a couple who married after meeting via the web, but the husband turned out to be a bit of a liar and cheat and that is mostly why I had my doubts. Now, I am throwing caution to the wind.

You stated that you are single but had a relationship for over ten years, have grown children and were a single parent. That must have been a real challenge. I was always grateful I had my husband to turn to for support. Did you ever marry?

Living with monks also sounded interesting. Where was that? How come you wrote 'n/a' next to having a car? Do you only get around by bicycle or boat?

One big drawback is that the miles between us must be measured by the shortest route, which in our case is the water. How far can you sail that boat of yours? If you don't have a car it's going to be near impossible to meet.

At this point I'd rather meet than spend lots of time typing messages into this little box provided by POF.

Tell me what you think.

Katie

My message was sent off at 10 p.m., and nothing was received the next day. But on the following, my messages showed I had received something around 2 a.m. that morning. Tony must be a night owl, staying awake after some of his shows.

Hello Katie,

It's hard to use our energy to fill the boxes. . . the mind fills up with noise through the day and it's the noise that keeps us from being in the moment. . .what I learned from the monks around the world on different occasions. Fear is noise and we should be proactively quiet.

I never married because I never saw the point of dragging the church or government into a love affair. . .not wise or beneficial. . .old school now and more a business deal. . . most people don't want to marry but for the gays and they get shit over it.

The question about having a car was an odd one in this day and age and sadly I've had one since age 15. . . but the bike riders smoking cigarettes are probably DUIers, not health nuts. I could bike to your place and bike over 100 miles weekly.

I've performed near you. Today was spent with a new singer making a promotional recording. We are already the best duo in the area but have only been together three months, aiming to do parties where we get over $100 per hour each, which is good income and good for the ego.

My boat is ocean worthy, world class and very fast. I can park it around as a night spot and getaway.

I don't mind writing since I'm a fast typist, but feel free to call me if you wish at 917-891-7276. I am up late, best to reach me after 9 p.m. on weekdays.

Blessings,

Tony

A couple of things struck me about his note. Even if he sounded unconventional, he still seemed to be like-minded, and the thought of going to clubs and restaurants to listen to him play struck me as very appealing. Many men listed various television programs as their main interests and that appeared boring, even if truthful. He was definitely a doer, not a watcher, and I could almost envision sailing off in his ocean-ready sailboat with cool breezes caressing my face.

Nonetheless, I still didn't take him seriously, and another week went by before I thought too much about contacting him. But, when the realization set in that Bill was not calling anymore I decided to reach out to Tony. It was one of those evenings while I lounged in bed prior to bedtime with the phone nearby, just in case, when I realized I had to do something for myself to get out of the waiting-for-him to call again mode.

I checked online and dialed the number Tony had provided.

"Hello," a boyish male voice answered.

"Hello, is this Tony Dylan?" I asked.

"Yes."

"This is Katie, the woman you corresponded with on Plenty of Fish. You know, you're one of the few men who use their real names."

"I don't see how it matters much," he said.

"Thank you for providing your telephone number. I was looking over your profile and thought I'd just call to let you know that I think we really don't have much in common, but I find you interesting nonetheless."

He laughed. "There's only so much that can be written," he said.

"True, and even then most of that can be deceptive."

"I remember your profile. You're the woman who wants to see how relationships progress naturally. You sounded very philosophical."

"That's right. I did study philosophy in college, which prepared me for law school. A philosophy major has absolutely no marketable skills to offer out in the workforce. There was no choice—since I couldn't get a job I had to go back to school. Funny though, sometimes pursuing something just because it's fascinating, even if not practical, is the best thing that can happen to you in life."

"You are right indeed," he replied. "I followed Spinoza, myself." Tony had a lyrical quality to his voice and a certain youthfulness which sounded very soothing, yet exciting. I couldn't remember Spinoza's tenets offhand—I thought he might have been looking for God in nature—but wasn't ready to disclose that I had already forgotten what I had learned in college.

"Tell me more about your music," I diverted the conversation to something practical.

"I've been playing since I was a kid and really enjoy it. I've been over to your island many times. The female I just hooked up with though is sometimes off key and I'm looking for more solo jobs. I was hired for a kid's birthday party and am having a hard time figuring out how to keep youngsters entertained for two hours."

"How old will the children be?" I asked, while silently noting that his relationship with his singing partner, which he had indicated was so great, had already taken a nose dive. It was not a good sign.

"The kids will be in the under age seven category."

"That's a difficult group to keep engaged for a length of time."

"That's why the parents hire me!" he acknowledged.

"You could do some sing-alongs and other activities that actively engage them in your act."

"Let's face it—kids are the toughest to entertain."

"I agree," I said, "although little do I know about it Adults will just tune you out if they're not engaged in your act. Little ones will act out and let you know they're not impressed!"

We laughed heartily and the conversation flowed easily.

"How often do you go camping?" I asked, referring to the *Interests* section of his profile.

"I haven't camped in awhile, but did when I went exploring the United States," he said.

"Well, my idea of camping is hiking in the woods by day and settling into a cabin with electricity and running water by night," I said. "In fact, that's the closest I've ever come to the experience, and doubt that I would ever try a sleeping bag and tent and this stage in my life."

"I plan to take my sailboat and use it as my lodging in due course," Tony said.

"That sounds really exciting. I know a couple who do live off of their boat for months at a time."

"That's the plan," he said. "I haven't exactly gone far yet, but once I get the boat in shape I want to head south and make it to the Keys."

His mention of getting his boat in shape did not exactly fit with his description of having an ocean ready vessel. Making it to the Keys would involve sailing south on the Gulf Coast of Florida. I didn't comment.

"What is the 'food science' you also mention as one of your many interests?" I asked instead.

"Well, for example, for breakfast I take some ice, banana, yogurt, wheat germ, fiber and a bit of spice and blend it up to make what is the perfect meal," he explained. A liquid diet did not exactly appeal to me, so I said nothing but, "that sounds nutritious."

"For two people who have little in common we certainly have plenty to talk about!" I said.

"Whenever you feel like talking, just give me a call. As I said, I'm usually in after 9 p.m. unless I have a job."

"Thanks. It's been fun talking to you." I said as I hung up the phone while noticing the clock, which indicated that we'd been chatting for over an hour.

The next morning my phone rang with a message that I was receiving a text to landline. It was from Tony saying, "Good morning gorgeous." It certainly got my day off to a good start, even though we had yet to meet so he couldn't tell exactly what I looked like. Photos alone could be very deceiving. I had no desire to call him back immediately since the day was already full of activities.

The week flew by because of my busy schedule; swinging the wooden ping pong-like paddle used in pickleball involved just the right level of exertion to strengthen the upper arms; biking to and from the Center was an adequate warm up and cool down, followed by the quick dip in the Bay before showering, lunching and taking the afternoon siesta. Afterwards, it was practically dinnertime, and cool enough to get Trooper running alongside the bicycle for his daily workout. On Sunday afternoon the Center was closed and I was feeling low. Tony had told me to call him whenever, and so I placed a call. He picked up on the second ring and once we got started chatting the hours flew by. He was so amazingly easy to talk to, I thought. We never seemed to run out of things to say.

"Look," Tony said finally, "we've been on the phone for three hours. Let's take this to the next level and meet."

"Any idea where?" I asked.

"Why don't we meet somewhere in the middle?"

I looked at Google maps. "How about downtown Bradenton on the pier? It's about a 30 to 40 minute drive for each of us. There's a casual riverfront restaurant on the pier that's nice."

"I can leave in 20 minutes," Tony said.

"I can leave in an hour," I promised.

"I'll wait," he said.

I took a quick shower and changed my outfit. In 30 minutes I was ready to go. I called Tony back.

"Yes ma'am," he answered coldly.

"I'm just calling to say I'm ready to go."

"Good! I thought you were calling because you had second thoughts," Tony said. The marked enthusiasm in his voice was undeniable.

"How will I recognize you?" I asked.

"I'll be wearing white slacks and a black and white striped shirt."

Off I went after throwing Trooper a few extra biscuits as a special treat. When I pulled into the parking area I found a space close to the river front. As I exited the car I spotted a youngish looking man walking directly in front of the car. He was wearing white slacks but a navy blue and white shirt so I assumed it wasn't Tony, but couldn't be sure.

"Are you Tony?" I called out.

'No, but I just passed a guy back there who was looking for someone," he said.

"Really?" I asked.

He approached me and took my hand in his.

"Will you marry me?" he asked very seriously.

I laughed out loud, and said, "I thought it was you but for the wrong color shirt."

"You mean this isn't black?" he asked.

His outfit looked casual and trendy. On closer inspection I noticed the button down shirt had nice details to it—small pearl buttons on the sleeves and a ribbed round collar that opened. When I glanced down at his slacks I noticed that they were fairly heavily stained. White was the toughest color to wear. But if I had time to shower and change, why hadn't he, I wondered.

We couldn't quite decide where to sit. He suggested the outdoor patio, but it was too hot. We tried the bar, but it was too noisy. The covered patio was too crowded. We ended up in the formal dining room but when the hostess said there would be a bit of a wait he seemed to get upset and did a turn around, walking off and away from me a few steps. I thought it was a bit of an extreme reaction to having to wait a few minutes for a table. It appeared he got frustrated easily, and that reminded me of Scott. It was not a pleasant memory of unpredictable but regular temperamental outbursts.

Once seated, at a table set for four with an elegant white tablecloth and cloth napkins rolled in metal napkin holders, Tony was calm again. We had arrived in time for happy hour and were glad to order off of the reduced price menu that was still in effect for the next ten minutes. I noticed that Tony ordered wine even though his profile claimed he did not drink. Once we relaxed sipping on our drinks, Tony asked, "Do you think I look 55?"

"Yes, you do. I do not feel like I am robbing the cradle," I replied.

"Well I'm really older than you," he said.

I sat quietly, not knowing what to say. Why were men lying about their ages, which had always been a characteristic of older women?

"Don't you want to know?" Tony asked.

"Sure, how old are you really?" I asked, trying to mask my annoyance.

"I'm 62."

"You don't look it," I said honestly. If I looked as good as he did I would have been bragging about it. "Tell me more about your education. What was your major?"

"Oh, I only went for a semester or so."

I was flabbergasted. He purported to be a college graduate, but was a college drop out! This really bothered me--the lies were growing and growing and soon nothing would be believable I feared.

"You know, Tony, we are really coming from different backgrounds. I have led a completely conventional life, that embraced marriage and organized religion, while you took the road less traveled," I commented. "I still go to mass on Sundays."

"As long as you don't expect me to attend with you it wouldn't matter," he said.

"I've never had to tie someone up and drag them off to church with me!" I countered, but silently thought how much more comfortable I would be with someone who shared my faith, even if he didn't practice it regularly in a church setting. To be a "free thinker" left me wondering exactly what he did believe.

"How is your son doing?" I asked, referring to the child he said he raised alone.

"I haven't heard from him in ages and am not sure where he is," Tony admitted, not sadly, but as a statement of fact. Since it had just been Father's Day, I considered this odd and sad indeed. Although none had sent gifts, all of my children at least called to talk with me on Mother's Day.

"I home schooled him," Tony said.

"Really! I couldn't wait to find all the best schools for my kids so I could ship them off for the day," I said, while wondering how competent a high school graduate was to home school a child. The thought made me feel critical and judgmental of him, but I thought it nonetheless.

We enjoyed our appetizers, and treated them like dinner. When the waitress presented the bill I took out my wallet and offered to pay my share.

"Why don't you get the tip," Tony suggested. I complied without comment and was glad I didn't have to feel entirely beholden to him for the mini meal.

We left the dining room and found an oversized upholstered chair in the lobby where we could both sit together. He began to massage my back. It felt good. Then I realized how odd it might look to the passing patrons, that these two older people were engaging openly in physical contact in public.

"I should be on my way," I said. "It looks like the restaurant in closing soon."

"I enjoyed meeting you," Tony said.

"It's been fun," I agreed.

When Tony tried to call me a few times in the following days, and sent an email asking me to contact him, I ignored his messages. I could not believe he was about to start living in a world he had rejected his entire life. One day I noticed he had deleted me from his contacts online, and I was relieved.

Flipshot

The more I thought about Bill, the more I wished he would call again. Just talking on the phone with him had been lively and entertaining. It seemed to me that we were very similar in many ways: a materialistically poor childhood followed by a more successful adulthood. Of course Bill's career had been far more successful financially, but he must be used to being rather alone in that class. We both had long term marriages but his ended in divorce while mine had ended with a death. We both practiced our faith, or at least he indicated he did.

Then again, talking with Tony was entertaining as well. But Tony could not to be taken seriously even if he thought he should be. When I sounded out my islander advisory board about whether I should contact Bill again, the consensus seemed to think not; I should just let it be. Many women believed that men still preferred to be the pursuers, and that if he had to be pursued he wouldn't be worth pursuing. I wasn't sure I agreed with that, but was willing to bow to public opinion, that being the consensus of twelve women having coffee together.

To take my mind off of Bill I went back online and reviewed my matches and prospects, most of whom had stayed the same, but some new profiles seem to have been added. Diamonds4u was still among my top ten. The *Meet me* feature was tried, which displayed photos of men with whom you had to choose whether you would want to meet or not. As each photo was displayed there was a link to his profile so I spent an hour checking out these new prospects, marking "yes, I'd like to meet him," for about two, "no, I would not want to meet him," for about six, and "maybe, I'd like to meet him," for another two.

Before I signed off for the night, a message came in from Flipshot,

Where is Anna Maria Island? I live in Sarasota near Siesta Key.

Thank you,

 Flip

Flip had been one I indicated I would like to meet. I clicked back over to his short, succinct profile:

    62-year-old, 5'9", Christian, animal lover, has dog, grey eyes

    Divorced; had been involved over 10 years; wants a dating relationship

    Graduate degree, retired

    Interested in sports, exercise and food

    New to area, likes to play and watch golf; hates to eat alone

Flipshot sounded just fine to me. Having someone to have meals with would go a long way for filling in those long lonely evening hours.

I responded within 15 minutes of getting his message.

We are practically neighbors. Anna Maria is north perhaps 20-30 miles, depending on exactly where you are, 30-60 minutes depending on traffic.

I noted that he was still online as I sent the message.

He immediately responded.

Maybe we can meet somewhere in the middle. The snowbirds are gone; maybe the traffic will be lessened.

I could suggest a location.

St. Armand's or Coquina Beach are somewhere in between us, and are a very pretty drive.

The chat continued.

I like the water. Is there a place at Coquina Beach to have a drink and eat?

I wondered if that query represented an actual invitation.

Yes, there's some type of concession. What are you doing tomorrow in the late afternoon?

He responded:

My house is being renovated, so any excuse to get out is good. I just need directions and a time.

I was certainly pleased to have gotten this far with him this quickly. I responded immediately.

Let's plan to meet at the concession at Coquina Beach at 5 p.m. Take the Gulf of Mexico Drive north, cross out of Longboat Key, and pull into the main lot on your left. I'll wear my swimsuit.

P.S. It's too bad dogs aren't permitted there.

His acknowledgement was instantaneous, as though he was waiting and watching his computer screen.

That's ok. He doesn't own a suit.

See you at five.

I couldn't quite follow why he said his dog didn't own a swimsuit, but it struck me as rather funny. I settled back in bed, contented that I had something to do the next afternoon. While signing off, I remarked that our online conversation had spanned not quite 45 minutes. I was perfecting how to move things along at a rapid pace. After all, wasn't everyone's primary goal a first meeting?

The next day I stayed busy having coffee with the islanders, taking a pilates class and hanging out afterwards with Jane while the Center was being filmed for a promotional piece on YouTube. At home I felt entitled to eat a sandwich for lunch, make a 100 calorie bag of kettle corn and settle in to watch an afternoon movie.

Netflix seemed to have less and less that interested me, with the foreign films tending to be the ones that I ended up enjoying most. The license to display them must be less expensive than getting second rate American films.

Trooper was fed early and taken for a quick run. Since the afternoon heat was still bearing down even the dog did not want to run far. I jumped into the Bay, then showered off quickly outside, changing out of the wet suit and into a dry one. I sprayed all exposed areas of my body with sun block. There was no use putting on much makeup if we intended to go swimming in the Gulf, so I just lightly coated my upper eyelids with a smoky colored eye shadow that seemed to make my blue eyes stand out more, and then applied several layers of lipstick. I wondered what Flip's alleged gray eyes would look like, and could not recall anyone having that color.

This would be my first date that was going to be a walk on the beach, which was a choice many people made when describing their idea of a good first date. I got into the car at 4:30 p.m. and made it to Coquina Beach 10 minutes early. I positioned myself where I could see the cars that were entering the park. There were virtually none, and the expansive parking lots were practically empty. A small gray car entered and pulled in behind a waiting bus. As if realizing that it was just a circle for buses to collect and discharge passengers, the older dented Malibu backed out slowly until it could turn into the parking lot. There was a man behind the wheel and I thought that must be Flip.

I moved over to stand in front of the concession building. There was no one else there to compare me with, so Flip should have no trouble spotting me. I pulled out a small cardboard sign with his name printed on it and held it up—a bit of a joke, but maybe an easy identifier. He walked over towards me and said, "Katie, how are you?" He made no remark about the makeshift sign.

"Did you have any trouble finding your way here?" I asked.

"No, the coastal route was quick and easy," he replied.

"Why don't we sit on the beach?" I asked, and we walked together across the expansive beach moving closer to the water's edge. There were only handfuls of people on the beach under the dark threatening late afternoon rain clouds, so no matter where we went we would be enjoying relative privacy.

"Can you get the umbrella?" I asked. Flip proceeded to open and install the beach umbrella deep into the sand, while I got out an old cotton tablecloth I had packed in the beach bag and spread it out for us to sit on. He kept the umbrella open just a few feet off of the ground, so we both somewhat crawled to get underneath it. We were totally protected from the sun's rays. He sat on the far edge of the cloth, and the umbrella pole separated us. He faced away from the water.

"Don't you want to look out over the water?" I inquired. I couldn't imagine anyone at the beach looking back to the parking lot instead of the water.

"It's fine."

"Tell me, how did you come by your online name, 'Flipshot?'" I asked, while taking note that his eyes were a light blue.

"It's my name," he answered.

"Do you mean to tell me that if I looked at your birth certificate it would say 'Flipshot?' " I asked.

"Well no. My name is Philip, but everyone used to shout it out so quickly that it began to sound like "flip" so that's how I got it. The "shot" I added when I engaged in a venture by that name."

"Tell me more about yourself. Your profile said you recently moved here and you love golf."

"Right," he said. "I moved here when my wife and I divorced two years ago after 37 years of marriage. I live in a condo that my parents had owned and that my sister and I inherited after their deaths. I do play golf almost every morning and watch tournaments on TV in the afternoons."

His description of his day sounded rather monotonous, but not too different from they way I might describe my own, as alternating from the gym, to swim, to rest with a movie in the afternoon.

"Tell me; is 62 your real age? I've been finding many men have been reporting their ages incorrectly."

"Of course," he responded, looking a bit bewildered, as if not understanding why anyone would lie.

"I think some men want to attract younger women, so they say they are younger," I said. It was a plus for him that it had never occurred to him to lie.

"What kind of work did you do before you retired?" I asked.

"My father started a very successful family business selling commercial stoves to customers worldwide. I got to travel extensively abroad to meet the customers. Then, the Japanese came out with a much better product and our business suffered. My father died. I sold the business for just pennies on the dollar of its former worth."

Flip did not present the image of a successful businessman, but I felt sorry for his plight, which seemed to be no fault of his own.

"Afterwards, I put my money into a deal that I called a 'one-shot' business, but it was a bit of a scheme which backfired and I lost my money," he continued.

I sat quietly, digesting his bad news.

"Then, I drove a limo and had fun meeting famous people." Flip rattled off the names of some of the people he had driven, but it still seemed to me that driving a car was a real comedown for someone who had been engaged in international travel as a part of his normal business routine.

"When that business dried up I ended up being at home while my wife worked. Her elderly father moved in with us and I took care of his needs, shopped and attended to home repairs. Suddenly my wife asked for a divorce. I wanted to wait until our two boys had finished college, but then we just went ahead and did it. She got the house, and I got a portion of her retirement fund. I doubt that she will ever retire," he lamented.

"Eventually she'll have to," I said. "I'd like to take a dip," I said to change the subject. I got up, removed my beach robe and walked towards the Gulf.

He got up and walked alongside me. As he was crawling out from under the umbrella I noticed he had brown staining in the middle rear of his shorts. He would be the second date to arrive wearing stained, dirty clothing. "I was hoping you'd wear your swimsuit," I said.

"I thought I wrote and told you I didn't have one, or if I did I wasn't able to find it," he said.

"I understood that to mean you were referring to your dog," I replied.

He looked at me in a quizzical way. I ran into the surf and waded out until I could immerse my body. The water was so warm that it wasn't even refreshing. He stood on shore looking out towards me. I didn't even try to swim, so made my way out after just a few minutes. It seemed rude to have him just standing there alone on the beach.

I sloshed back to shore looking into the ridged bottom of the Gulf while looking out for stingrays, and wished I had something with which to cover the loose baggy skin of my thighs. We began to walk along the shore.

"I may be giving up my beagle soon," Flip said.

"How old is he?" I asked.

"He's eight. I adopted him from a vet school and he had had his vocal cords removed."

"The most distinctive thing about a beagle is that howl!"

"Well, he's a quiet one now but he can make some gurgling type sound. He's really making it hard for me to travel."

"I know. I have the same problem with my dog, Trooper. He's also eight," I commiserated. Silently I was horrified. How could he describe himself as an animal lover, then talk about giving his dog the death penalty because the dog crimped his travel plans? Shouldn't he have considered that eight years ago when he adopted the dog? No one would want to adopt an aging dog without vocal cords.

"I was able to find a neighbor who comes by the house and takes care of my dog when I travel," I said. "It's much less expensive than the vet's office."

"I'm planning to be gone for many weeks in the next coming months. I don't want to take the dog with me," Flip said.

"I just plan to take longer road trips and go places where the dog is welcome or can stay for a nominal fee," I said. I suddenly felt the need to change the topic to something less upsetting. "How are you doing on Plenty of Fish?"

"I've had about five dates in Florida in the past one and one-half years," he said.

"Really, I've had that many in the past month," I exclaimed. I wasn't going to tell him he was actually my ninth date and I had another date for a drink lined up for the upcoming weekend. "But," I explained, "I've been working at it and looking every day."

"I don't look unless I'm notified I got a message," Flip said.

"Well then, that's why."

We circled back to where the cloth was. Gulls had come and seemed to be pecking at it. They were shooed away. Flip took down the umbrella and I shook out the cloth, folded it up and put it away in the beach bag. We walked over to my car and deposited the goods inside, then headed down the graceful tree lined path towards the pass between Coquina and Longboat Key.

"A little boy was swimming off this point last year, was swept off by the current and drowned," I remembered out loud. "Look, there are plenty of signs posted showing to beware of the rip current. It was such a needless tragedy."

"I hadn't heard about it," he answered.

"What did you get your graduate degree in?" I asked.

"I got a bachelor's from the local college."

"But your profile says you have a graduate degree," I insisted as if he had to be wrong about his own history.

"I just meant I graduated from college, meaning 'graduate' degree," he said.

I said nothing but wondered if he was trying to be funny or was just stupid. We headed back towards where the cars were parked.

"How about going for a drink?" he offered.

"Sure," I said, but was not too enthused. By 7 p.m. the concession was closed for the night. We went to our cars. "Follow me," I instructed, "there are lots of places just about a mile north of here."

"Lead the way," he said.

He certainly was agreeable, and easy to talk to as well. It just was unfortunate that not much of what he had to say was that impressive. He was just content to meander through his days playing golf. He wasn't asking for much from a woman, merely a dinner date, and at this point that sounded quite appealing.

I led the way up to the Tiki Hut on Gulf Drive where the food was mediocre but reasonably priced, the view of the Gulf was terrific and sometimes there was live music. Once there I requested a change of table twice. The first table was in direct sunlight and was blinding. The second table was swarming with tiny black ants because someone had tried to use sugar packets to even out the table top.

"I used to drive my husband crazy," I said. "I was always finding fault with hotel rooms and requesting a different one for one reason or another."

Flip suggested we get some food as well, and ordered the Caesar's salad that I ought to have ordered. I ordered a hamburger and fries. I hadn't eaten meat in over a week. When I went out with Bill and Tony we'd had fish entrees. When the food was served I noticed a slightly off taste to the burger when I bit into it. I ate it nonetheless, not wanting to make a big deal out of it, especially after changing tables so many times. Later that night, sick in the bathroom, I was sorry I hadn't sent it back to the kitchen.

"You know, I like to write," Flip said. "I was told it could be very therapeutic to combat depression." I wondered if he said that to acknowledge he suffered from depression. "Every day I write in a notebook and list everything I have done. I have kept all of my notebooks and wonder what my children will do with them after I die." He proceeded to pull out a tiny 25 cent type 2x4" spiral bound notepad. He flipped it open and it showed a list of four items:

> *golf,*
>
> *lunch,*
>
> *drive,*
>
> *Coquina.*

"I don't see where our meeting is noted," I said.

"It's here," he said pointing with his finger, "Coquina." It didn't strike me as though his notebooks were ever going to find much literary value.

When the bill came I placed a $20 bill on the table and said, "Let me contribute towards this."

Flip pushed it back and said, "It's okay, I can get this."

"If I had known that I would have taken you somewhere more expensive," I teased.

"I'm usually good for two dates," he said. "That's about my limit."

I thought of the two dates I had with Bill, and the third date I couldn't schedule with him. Maybe Bill felt the same way. We walked back towards our cars and didn't kiss or shake hands good bye.

"Thanks for a fun evening. What if I want to contact you again?" I asked.

"Try my email —Flipshot@gmail.com," he suggested.

I didn't need to write that down. I doubted I would be contacting him again. His comment about wanting to get rid of his dog because it crimped his travel plans bothered me, even though I remembered last year when I considered giving Trooper to my cousin who said she would take Trooper anytime.

But then, my cousin had offered to take Trooper without my having to ask.

I was really grossed out that Flip wore dirty clothes to our first date, and drove a dented car.

Even though it might not be fair, these first impressions clouded my opinion of him and made him unattractive. His career, by his own admission, had been a failure. It was depressing to think about losing everything for which you worked. There was just something insipid about Flip—he was pleasant enough to be with, but seemed like he was accustomed to, and content with, the mediocre.

I felt exhausted by all of these men I was finally meeting and dating. Yet it was everything I had been praying for just a few weeks earlier! I still felt empty and alone, and couldn't figure why I was finding fault with so many of them when they were complimentary and treating me well.

The only two of the six men I would have liked to become more serious with—SarasotaBill and Diamonds4u--were no longer interested in me.

I was fairly certain that there was no future with the other men I had met. Benjamin was not ready for the long term permanent relationship he claimed to want. The huge legal bills, contested divorce and alimony due his ex-wife left him financially as well as emotionally drained. He wasn't ready to trust a woman again. He was lonely, and like me, disliked the reality of living alone after decades of being in the company of other family members. It was going to take him time to accept what he had, find satisfaction with his decision and become emotionally stable enough to engage in another relationship.

In every relationship there always was one person who seemed to want it more, or be more emotionally enthusiastic than the other, and that's how it was with Hugh and Bill.

I was impressed by them and had been willing to make more aggressive moves and take charge of moving things along. But I couldn't do it all alone, and neither seemed to be as interested as I was. It was more likely than not that Hugh was already involved with someone else, remembering how he called off our second date at the last moment.

Bill knew how to wine and dine a woman, but was not actively courting me. The age difference was noticeable to me, more so because he had not acknowledged it, even if we didn't present like father and daughter in public.

Eliot had been the most promising date, based on his correspondence and telephone calls. He was eager to keep up messaging and loved to talk on the phone about anything and everything. In person he presented himself as insecure and nervous, and although I knew it was petty, I held it against him that he hadn't paid for our meal or taken me out to eat the way he promised he would.

The old adage, "you only get one chance to make a good first impression," rang true.

I could have imagined sailing off into the sunset with Tony and smiled when I thought of his marriage proposal, after a lifetime of being single, but I never believed he could really change the behavior of a lifetime just for me. Maybe I was wrong though; maybe he was looking to change his life and ready to start a new one. I knew I had hurt his feelings by ignoring his calls and messages, but the cowardly approach of a clean break was all I could manage. Maybe it would be easier for him, to have a reason to dislike me.

Surfman

I went back online to Plenty of Fish, to use again the feature called *"Meet Me"*, in which an array of men's photos would flash on the screen, and I could mark whether or not I would be interested in meeting that person. It epitomized judging someone solely by his looks as depicted in his posted photo, which could be a very unfair way of picking a mate, especially one who didn't photograph well. Nonetheless it was very entertaining, and I could pass agreeable hours sifting through the profiles annexed to the pictures, considering all the seemingly endless possibilities for a future date and mate.

I wasn't running across as many that I wanted to follow up with employing the technique of weeding out the undesirables, which included eliminating any man whose profile contained the following information:

I do not drink

Longest relationship under 10 years

High school education or some college

Under 5'7" tall

Never married

Body type overweight, i.e., big & tall

Seeking only dating

I wasn't sure that just because a man never drank it necessarily meant that he was on the wagon and had an issue with alcohol, but I was fairly sure the majority of men would fit that category. I didn't want someone shorter than me, and it was just a personal bias.

Why a man would indicate he only wanted to date was a mystery to me, but if he never wanted to progress from that superficial state, maybe he was still married. I just wasn't interested.

I forgot that my original profile had indicated that I was just interested in dating, and that I had marked that since it seemed to be the precursor to any relationship. I yearned for the intellectual stimulation a college educated man would be more likely to provide. If he had never married and was within my preferred age range of 50 – 70 years, it was unlikely he would ever consider marrying me, and I wanted that option left open even though I had no desire to remarry in the foreseeable future. If a man didn't keep himself in shape and indicate he had at least an "average" body type, I didn't want to be the one to put him on a diet, even if I could imagine how delicious it might be, being nourished from kisses alone.

The *profile* of a candidate who named himself Surfman caught my eye, initially because he was also a resident of the island and Google maps put his location at just one-half of a mile away. Even though it stated he wanted to date, his intent was listed as a long term relationship. His other particulars were okay:

Drinks socially

66-years-old, 5'8", athletic body type, blond hair

Divorced with longest relationship over 10 years

Masters degree, profession—beach bum

It struck me funny that he would designate himself a beach bum, and defined it as one who "collects bottles for nickels." Surfman also had the longest lists of *interests* I had ever seen—over thirty, and some were really cute:

You

Mexican food

Car shows

Neal Preserve

Boating; especially sailing into the sunset with you

Parasailing

Tennis

Affection

Florida

Cooking a meal for you

Sailing into the sunset with you

Amusement theme parks

Rock n roll

Rafting

Paddleboards

Basketball

Reggae music

Beaches

One man boats

Weekend trips

Being outdoors

Hiking

Seafood

Horseshoes

Fishing

Fishing from the piers

Fishing expeditions

Soccer

Bicycling

Romancing you

Camping

Cinemas

Science

Shopping in thrift stores

You guessed it--surfing

It was obvious the man had a well developed sense of humor, and had fully embraced island life. He must have tried to list every activity he ever enjoyed, but I found it fresh and imaginative, rather than trying to sort through some men's abbreviated list of four or five items which presented a fairly drab picture and didn't give a girl much to work with in terms of planning a date. Surfman would be an easy man to entertain---just walk him on the beach and hand him a fishing pole or surf board!

His *Description* of himself also showed promise of a well developed sense of humor:

What about me? Wrong . . . this is all about us and what we like and may enjoy doing together. We should both be honest, sincere, extroverted, affectionate, monogamous, joyful, Christian, clever, athletic, talkative, and passionate. If you don't have all of these qualities then let's not waste each other's time. Okay, if you have four of these qualities we really ought to meet. If you have at least two of these qualities please send me a message. If you have only one, and that one is 'sincere' please consider contacting me immediately because we probably have more in common than you think. PLEASE give me a chance! Even if you think we have absolutely nothing in common you may be wrong. I will take all inquiries seriously and will respond to everyone who bothers to write!

I've been on this dating site for years now and my health is rapidly declining. Get me while I'm still walking without a cane! I've had only two hospitalizations in the past four months and take only ten medications daily. I am the most serious candidate on Plenty of Fish and know how to take good care of a woman. I have lots of money, and hope you do too!

I want to sail out onto the Gulf with you by my side. Don't worry; I am a world champion sailor even if you don't know how. I can take care of us!

Trust me, or if that's too soon at least give me a chance to prove myself to you.

Most relationships deteriorate for lack of good communication but don't even have a chance if you don't start tapping on your keys to send me a message, flirt, indicate you want to meet me, or just mark me as a favorite. If I don't respond within 24 hours then just forget me, but once you meet me I promise it will be unforgettable.

Similarly, his description of his idea of a good *First Date* was entertaining:

Isn't that why we are here? Let's not waste anymore time. I just need about 15 minutes to see if there is any chemistry between us. Let's pick a point that's halfway for each of us. You name the place! It can be a park, museum, pier, beach, aquarium, restaurant, sporting venue, hiking trail, e.g. Anywhere you say is okay with me as long as it's not McDonald's, Starbucks, Wendy's, Burger King, Kentucky Fried Chicken, Olive Garden, or Dairy Queen. Five Guys or Chipotle would be okay with me, but you decide what you like best. My treat. It's all up to you now. I have only one requirement: you must be the same person who's in your profile's photo!

A few weeks back Surfman had marked me as one of his *Favorites*, which was enough of a sign from him. I wrote back to him:

Surfman,

Let's plan a rendezvous at the Gulf front park at 6 p.m. tonight. Apparently you need to schedule a mere 15 minutes for the initial chemistry test.

Hope you can make it!

Katie

Surfman must have been at his computer and online too, because his answer was sent right back:

You're on. I think I can find the park since it's only two blocks away. I'm nervous though and feel more at ease on a starting line with 40 boats waiting for the gun! It's nice to be around the corner so to speak.

Unlike most of the other dates, I didn't bother to prepare in any special way for the meeting with Surfman. It was all about the casual beach, so there really wasn't anything to do but decide what pair of sandals to wear. I could bike over to the park.

When I got there I spotted a man bearing his resemblance sitting on the park bench. I drifted over to him.

"Do I have the pleasure of meeting Surfman?" I asked.

"Katie, I presume. I'm so glad you made it," he said. He had a big smile on his face, which I had noticed with men who were genuinely pleased with my appearance.

His appearance, unfortunately, wasn't too attractive. He was slender and athletic, but his face looked far older than 66; it looked positively ancient. The years spent on the beach had done considerable damage, with deep lines etching his skin throughout. It was not kissable skin material. His hair was light, but had no remaining blond strands that I could discern.

"You were easy to spot. Tell me, when you wrote that you wanted the person whose photo was posted did you imply that sometimes someone else showed up for the date?" I asked in all seriousness.

"Many women post photos from years ago and they no longer really look like that. You, however, look better than your photo and that is truly rare!" Surfman said.

I felt warm from his obvious pleasure with my appearance. We chatted on the park bench for a bit.

"Would you like to head over to the pier for drinks?" he asked.

"Sure," I responded. "It looks like I made it past the initial vital 15 minutes to determine whether there was any chemistry between us!" I noted.

He laughed. He had also arrived on bicycle. The ride to the pier only took a few minutes. The bar area was fairly empty.

"Tell me more about your sailing career," I asked.

"I was world champion in 1995. Since then I've taken many long trips and earn extra money giving sailing lessons. There's nothing I enjoy than spending a day out on the water." His love of the sun shone on his face.

"I also enjoy going to estate sales on weekends," I volunteered.

"Look at this shirt," he said standing up, turning around and modeling it. "It only cost a dollar at the thrift store. I can live on $20,000.00 a year by buying used things. I got my car from my brother's estate for a mere $800.00. I found a receipt that showed he had just put over $2,000.00 in repairs!"

I was not impressed. For some reason, even though I sometimes purchased used clothing and enjoyed it, I would never brag about it to anyone other than a sister or girlfriend. Getting a car for a song from a brother's estate also did not impress me but I couldn't figure out why since I would be happy too if I could buy a good car for so little. I thought his point was that it really took little to live well, but he came off as being cheap. We were more alike than I wanted to admit.

This sense of his frugality was emphasized when he invited me back to his place for dinner.

"I have some rice and beans I cooked up yesterday and have handy," he offered.

"Thanks, but I have a previous engagement," I lied. I really couldn't imagine a worse way to spend a first date. I was not going to go over to his place, which he had mentioned was one-half of a ground floor duplex.

"Call me if you'd like to get together again then," he suggested, writing his number on a scrap of paper.

"Alright, I will," I said with feigned sincerity. I had no intention of calling him.

Sarasota Bill

The next night while browsing online around 10 p.m., I noticed that Bill was online coincidentally with me. It had been over a week since I had last spoken to him. On a whim I decided to send him a quick message.

Dear Bill,

I just wanted you to know you were my best date ever! I miss talking to you. I hope you find the lady who thrills you.

Hugs,

Katie

I pressed the send message button and fell asleep with the phone beside me.

In the morning I decided it was time to revise my profile again. I no longer liked the philosophical sounding narrative on love, and also wanted to delete any mention of my career as a lawyer as it seemed to attract an element that might presume a greater wealth than what I had. I kept the *Headline*, "Expecting Lightning to Strike" but designated "retired" as profession.

I elaborated on my *Interests*:

Swimming daily

Travel far and near

Theater productions

Cuddling with you and watching a movie

Being wined and dined

Hiking with my dog

Pickleball

Mah jongg

Browsing museums

Estate sales

Staying healthy and fit

Making my man happy

Preserving my principal and principles

Kissing contests

Romantic evenings on the beach

My *Description* was kept to a bare minimum:

I am looking for a well educated man with a sense of humor, character, of means, and even temperament.

I am a very trusting person who will believe everything you tell me, go anywhere you want to go, and probably will want to try anything you like to do, after our first date.

For the description of the *First Date*, I wrote:

We meet at the police station, produce two photo IDs and have our fingerprints run for priors, outstanding warrants and aliases. We both voluntarily submit to a lie detector test to confirm the particulars of each of our profiles, with the understanding that two or more misstatements or omissions will bring an immediate end to the date. A detective conducts an intensive background check to verify our respective marriage and/or divorce records, birth records, death records (if relevant to surviving spouse status), lawsuits, judgments, liens, bankruptcies, property ownership records, while we patiently wait together, enjoying each other's company while doing nothing special, sipping coffee.

Just for fun, while waiting, we each pick one prior employer to call on the spur of the moment to ask for a character reference.

When all goes well we get to a doctor's office to have blood tests performed. We submit to a brief physical examination to confirm our weight is within a medically acceptable range, our blood pressure is within normal limits or is being properly treated, and our chests are clear. Since I am healthy, we discuss sympathetically any chronic condition you might have. We sign authorizations to allow each other access to psychiatric records and substance abuse treatment records, if any exist. Because I am currently medication free, your current medications, if any, are reviewed. You agree to be tested for any possible allergy to my dog. We agree to adjourn the first date pending the results of the blood work and allergy testing. We kiss, but it is not goodbye, but hopefully, au revoir.

When the satisfactory blood work and allergy testing results are in we eagerly resume our first date, greeting with a bear hug that takes our breath away, meeting at a lawyer's office to discuss our expectations concerning living arrangements and guidelines for a prenuptial agreement. We discuss how expenses are to be handled, and agree a pro rata division, based upon our respective means, is most fair.

To celebrate the finale of our blissful first date we head off for a travel agent and book a Viking River Cruise for our second date. When we are uncertain of which one, you insist I choose, because your new goal in life, like mine, is to make sure we are happy. A 15-day itinerary including Paris on the Seine to Prague is the one for us. Since it's a 2 for 1 special I get to go free!

It's a mystery to me why I haven't had any first dates lately.

I hoped this profile would attract more educated and humorous dating candidates. I was getting dismayed at the number of unemployed high school graduates who had been seeking me out. I wondered if anyone would find my description of a first date as funny as I hoped it was. I went about my daily routine and wasn't too surprised that no one seemed to be responding to the new profile.

After sunset as I prepared for bed following a run with Trooper and dip in the Gulf, I was pleasantly surprised to hear the phone ring about the time Bill used to call. Indeed, caller ID shouted out, "Call from Wm E Long". I grabbed the phone and snuggled into bed with it.

I answered the call by saying, "This is my lucky night!"

"Good evening to you too," Bill replied.

"How nice of you to call me again," I said. "Truly, I've had a very lucky day."

"Why so," he asked, capitulating to my need to talk.

"Beside the fact that you are calling me, I was able to talk my way out of

161

a speeding ticket on Pine earlier."

"What happened?"

"I was doing some fundraising for our Community Center and was rushing to get to an appointment to ask a local merchant if we could count on some help for our July fundraising effort. I saw the revolving headlights behind and as I was pulling over I realized I had left the house without my driver's license."

"That's not good."

"Right, so when the officer approached my car, introduced himself and asked for my documents, I could only confess, 'Officer I'm in big trouble! I left in a hurry to make a 1 p.m. appointment trying to fundraise for our Community Center and left without my wallet containing my license. What else have I done?' to which he replied, 'You were doing 35 in a 25 mph zone which carries a fine of $213.' He took my registration and insurance card, then returned and let me off with a warning!"

"My daughter was in traffic court today," Bill said, "trying to convince a hearing officer that she was not at fault for an accident which totaled her $50,000 car. She was making a left turn and was hit by an oncoming car."

"Usually the one who did not have the right of way is at fault."

"Her car had a black box which she produced to show that she was virtually out of the intersection when she was hit by the other car, which may have been oncoming from the shoulder."

"That may exonerate her."

"The decision will be in next week. But that's not why I am calling," Bill said. I enjoyed your note; it was the loveliest note I ever received."

"You must not receive many," I joked, trying to remember exactly what I said. Whatever it was had been short. It was not the rhyming verse I sent to Hugh.

"I'd like to take you out again," Bill said.

"As I recall, I owe you a picnic lunch. I assumed you were finally calling me to collect," I countered.

"Are you busy this weekend—Friday perhaps?" he asked.

"Saturday would be better; I hate being on the island on the busy weekends," I said.

"Alright, I'll call to confirm," Bill said.

"It really is delightful hearing from you again Bill. You are quite the character!"

"Is this the same person who wasn't sure what character meant a few weeks ago?" he teased. "By the way, I read your new profile and see now you want a man of character."

"I thought your request for a person of character would be a quality I should demand as well," I responded.

"You're not going to get any responses with your requirements for a first date—the trip to the police station, doctor's office, and travel agent," he warned.

"That's okay; I've gotten you to call again!"

"Sleep well, dear," he said as he hung up the phone. I rested peacefully that night, just as he had directed.

I did not hear from him again throughout the week, and hoped he would not forget about the date. On Friday I was really sorry I had postponed our date until Saturday because I had nothing planned and faced a long evening home alone with Trooper. Around 9 p.m. the telephone rang and caller ID announced it was Bill calling.

"Hello dear Bill," I answered the phone.

"How's my sweetheart?" Bill asked. He certainly knew how to make me feel good.

"I'm glad you're calling me," I said.

"I've been thinking about our date. How would you like to meet in Sarasota?" he asked.

"I don't see why not," I answered.

"You could come to my house and I can give you a tour of Sarasota. From there I know of a good restaurant in Venice where we can drive," he suggested.

"That sounds great! My only impediment is the dog who can't stay home alone for long periods of time," I answered. I was pleased that I would be able to see his house.

"How long is he okay?" Bill asked.

"He can certainly go through the night, so I would imagine six to eight hours during the day would be okay," I said.

"Well take him outside and squeeze him real good before you go," Bill instructed in a teasing way. "Otherwise you could leave him out around the pool area," he suggested.

I appreciated his offer to let me bring the dog along, but didn't think Trooper could be left outside in the Florida heat for very long. "I'll run him before I come over. What time would you like me?" I asked.

"Why don't we start about 4 p.m.?" he suggested.

"Good, I'll plan to leave after 3 p.m. and will give you a call once on the road," I said.

"Until tomorrow then," he said while hanging up.

I went to sleep feeling very calm and contented. Bill had a way of making me feel cherished and safe, which the younger men I had met did not. I was the one making the age difference the impediment, but it was obvious Bill had his doubts as well. If it hadn't been for my note he would not have called me again.

The next day I got to the gym in the morning, then took Trooper on a very long three mile run, bringing the dog home only when he was drooling, practically limping along and sure to pass out on his favorite chair for the day. Bill had said to dress casual, so I chose a short skirt that showed off my legs with a fitted spaghetti strap top.

I called Bill when I was ready to depart. "I'm on my way but just have two quick stops to make," I said. I didn't go into further detail. He didn't need to know I needed to get gas for the car or stop at the dollar store for another pair of reading glasses. I believed women needed to keep the illusion of romance as well, as much as possible. He did not ask, and I did not tell.

The drive went quickly and the neighborhood around the Ringling where he lived was impressive. I pulled the car into the driveway and approached a set of double French doors. He opened the door and graced me with a light hug.

"Is it okay that I parked here?" I asked, pointing to the car.

"Darling, consider that your spot," Bill replied. His response made me feel most welcome. He certainly had mastered how to make a woman feel special!

"Did you get your masters degree in courtship?" I asked.

He proceeded to give me the grand tour of his home, of which he was justifiably proud. The renovations he had planned and executed had practically doubled it in size. It had two bedrooms on the first floor, a new kitchen with a sign that said, 'If a house didn't have to have a kitchen this room wouldn't be here,' an office which he would not let me see claiming it was too messy, a dining area with French doors leading out to a small enclosed pool area, and a great room with French doors lining the walls on two sides giving it the semblance of grandeur. He pointed up a staircase and mentioned there was the master suite. We did not go there. In the added-on great room in front of a TV and fireplace there were two oversized leather recliner chairs. We sat down and chatted for a bit. It was obvious that he was quite comfortable. I took note that there was no way to cuddle up next to him, but he certainly was prepared to have someone by his side.

I scanned the room and took note of the various decorative items on the table tops and shelves. Some were exquisite, virtually works of art, and some were tacky, like fake flowers in a cheap vase. He had a collection of mini race cars which looked incongruous next to a baby grand piano, and was something you'd expect to see in a boy's bedroom.

"Do you play?" I asked, gesturing towards the piano.

"No, I just happened to raise my paddle at a charity auction at the wrong time and ended up buying it by mistake," he chuckled. "Do you know after an auction you only have a couple of hours to move your winning bid out? It was quite a feat to line up the movers and get it into the house."

"I had a baby grand that the children learned to play on in my living room in New York. I couldn't sell it and ended up giving it away to a neighbor. How long have you lived here?" I asked, changing the subject.

"I've been here long enough to want to move back to Bird Key," he answered, mentioning another very exclusive area of Sarasota. "I've been looking at a few houses there. My daughter thinks I should move into a ranch style house with only one floor." It sounded very appealing, even though there was nothing wrong with his current house. His children must be concerned about his living alone.

"Your neighborhood is quite lovely," I said.

"Let's go out and I'll give you the grand tour," Bill suggested.

"Are we taking the fancy car?" I asked, having noticed an SUV was also parked in the driveway.

"Sure thing. I just save the SUV to help neighbors move stuff," he joked.

Bill proceeded to show me the artsy downtown of Sarasota, the dog track, the Bay front area and then the houses he was interested in buying in Bird Key. I had seen most of the places already but enjoyed the tour. When he drove into the exclusive gated neighborhood the guard recognized him and waved him in.

He proceeded to drive to Venice after stopping for gas and to use the facilities. He left the car running at the gas station so I wouldn't get uncomfortable. I noticed that when he walked his limp didn't seem so pronounced, but his gait lacked a fluidity of movement. He filled his sports car with premium gasoline and I noted that it cost almost twice as much to fill as my car. As he stood outside the passenger window pumping the gasoline I noticed a stain on the front of his trousers.

After showing me the main street of Venice and its waterfront, Bill took me to the Crow's Nest, a restaurant where he had thoughtfully reserved a table for two in the fancier upstairs dining room which commanded stunning views of the waterways. He certainly knew how to wine and dine and woman! He ordered his usual scotch, I my red wine, prolonging the dinner date as much as possible. That evening he ordered steak and potatoes from the appetizer offerings; I stuck with a fresh fish entrée. After dinner we moved outdoors to an upstairs terrace to enjoy the sunset. A more romantic date was not imaginable.

On the way back Bill suggested that we stop at what he considered to be the best ice cream parlor in the area. I was too full to want more, and didn't mention that milk products tended to make me feel bloated and gassy. We drove on.

"You know, an attorney who took over a case I was last working on called the other day. I think he was calling about a referral fee he owes me. When that money comes in I want to take you out for dinner!" I said. Bill smiled, seemingly amused by the prospect.

Back at his house we stood on his driveway. I looked towards his house and pointed to an upstairs balcony where a light had been left on. "Is that where your bedroom is?" I asked.

"Yes," he said, without saying more.

I was somewhat relieved he wasn't suggesting we go back inside. It was late, and by the time I drove back to the island Trooper would need to be let out. The date had lasted six hours, seven if the drive home was counted, and the entire time had been very comfortable and agreeable.

"Is it going to be two weeks until you decide whether or not to call me again?" I asked.

He chuckled but said nothing more. I stepped forward and put my arms around his shoulders, hugging him close to me. At first he seemed to just stand there, but then his arms went around my waist and I experienced the tiniest bit of pressure. The hug felt weak, not like Hugh's passionate embrace, which had engulfed my body in his.

"Thank you for another wonderful evening Bill," I said in departing. While driving home I debated the odds of his ever calling again. I wasn't sure how I would bet on that one, but it seemed like a long shot.

Diamonds4u

As the days passed I thought I had my answer concerning Sarasota Bill's intentions. He did not call. There were no emails. It seemed obvious he was not going to take any further steps to pursue a relationship. I wondered if he had expected me to go up to his bedroom with him, but if that were so he certainly would have put a bit more pressure in his hug, or so I thought!

He had certainly given indications that his libido was still alive and well, but maybe he was an old school gentleman who waited until marriage to take his woman to bed. Because of his references to other girlfriends, and a prior live-in relationship that had lasted a couple of years, I doubted that this was the case. I was the one who most likely would be the one to hold out for an engagement or marriage, and since I felt I wasn't ready for another marriage maybe my sexual signals were ambivalent. Maybe he was waiting for me to make the first move!

Out of the blue an email from *POF* indicated that Diamonds4u had marked me as his *favorite*. I checked my calendar. It had been over a month since our date and even though I fantasized that someday he might contact me again, I had rather successfully dismissed that thinking as wishful and magical.

I was amazed he even remembered me, and then recalled our aborted second date after which I had written him off, assuming he was playing the field with several women simultaneously. I was excited and thrilled nonetheless and went off to the gym feeling more buoyant and youthful than I had in days.

I contemplated the options: I could ignore him and he would most likely and inevitably fade away; I could respond by indicating he was still a *favorite* with me, or I could forward the poem I had written in contemplation of a second date. I calculated the chances of merely indicating he was also a *favorite* with me were not likely to evoke any real response. I remembered that not that long after our first date I had again marked him again as a *favorite* and had heard nothing from him based on that alone. I decided that it wouldn't hurt to forward the poem that had been written but never sent.

I searched my drafts and found it. I reread it slowly, then decided there really was nothing offensive about it, and if he chose to ignore it he could and that would be that. Sending it via *POF* insulated it somewhat from a one-on-one personal experience, providing a certain layer of anonymity and protection. I had not told him my last name, address, email or telephone numbers. He had given me his telephone number, but I did not abuse the privilege of having it, nor was tempted to call him unless I felt fairly certain he was inclined to want to get together again.

I hoped he would enjoy the rhyming message. I was happy with most of the sentiments it expressed, especially the verse:

When I think of you I'm moved to rhyme,

You're a tune with a pleasing melody,

A poem that resonates in my mind;

Something I'd like to hear, see and feel another time;

You move me, Hugh, to the sublime.

When I wrote it, it reminded me of a Cole Porter song. There was something pleasantly lyrical about it. I waited until that evening when I was snuggled in bed, then posted it to him. 45 minutes later, at midnight, I had his response:

I was away visiting some of my kids for Father's Day

It would be fun to get together again

Plan to come over for a swim

. . . It looks like my bribing the computer programmer worked!

What day would you like?

Hugh . . . and many thanks for the creative note!

By midnight I had already turned off the lights and fallen asleep. The next day I headed out for coffee and the gym without checking my emails. When I got back I took a swim and shower, then sat down and was glad to see he had responded so quickly. I laughed over the line that he bribed the computer programmer to keep us among each other's top prospects. It felt good knowing he had enjoyed the message, and I took a moment to think first how I'd like to respond before posting a reply.

We really don't have to go to France

to explore a bit more of some romance

.

I always enjoy an evening on the beach;

somewhere easy for both of us to reach.

Sunday for the sunset around eight

suits me fine and would be just great.

I posted my reply on the half hour and within the half hour Hugh replied:

Do you realize how romantic you are?

Either that or you're a plagiarist.

Sunday night . . .

I usually hit Marina Jack's with my friends

How does Monday night work for you?

At first I was upset that he considered going to what was basically a bar with friends more important than meeting me. Then I remembered I had done that with Sarasota Bill, assuming another day's wait in meeting really wouldn't matter. I remembered I wanted Bill to know I had a life independent of dating. I didn't realize he might have interpreted it as a bit of a slight, and it struck me as a bit sad, since my real intention with Bill was just to get a date, being most impressed with him and wanting him to be impressed with me. Now I realized that when someone put me off it felt like a put down. Since Hugh was suggesting we meet next week there really was no need to respond immediately.

By 9 p.m. I went back online and saw that Hugh was also online coincidentally. I wrote:

Monday is alright.

Shouldn't you be out on a date tonight?

I wasn't too surprised that he did not respond to that inquiry. When I checked a second time I could see that he had clicked offline. Our date night was three days away and I wasn't going to obsess over it or him.

After all, I was just suggesting watching the sunset together, which I did every night with or without a date. I could still remember how disappointed I felt when the proposed second date had fallen apart at the last minute, and was determined that he was not going to hurt my feelings again. He may have been offended that I questioned why he was at home, presumably alone and online, on a Friday night, even though I too was at home alone on a Friday night.

Monday morning I went online only to see that Hugh had removed me from his *favorites* list. It was alarming to think that a simple inquiry concerning his being at home on a weekend could have upset him so much he had changed his mind entirely about me. If he were that sensitive and changeable it was certainly better to know it up front and be done with him before I became more emotionally involved.

Then, about 9:30 a.m. a message from Hugh was received:

What are you up to today?

Perfect day for a swim

I saw the message before I left for the gym and felt better that he was not sloughing me off because of a perceived slight. It struck me how odd it was; such a simple message from him could make me feel so good. I thought a response could wait until I got back from my morning workout. When I got home two hours later I wrote back to Hugh:

I am busy prepping for a very important date later today!

But I always have time for a swim

and can drop what I'm doing on a whim

unless you've already booked your day and gone away.

In which case . . . Will you meet me around eight, adjacent to the Sand Bar

where I'll be waiting nearby on a beach's bench, not too far?

I proceeded to shower, then found a response from Hugh waiting.

Or you could come down here anytime

A few minutes later another message came in,

Wouldn't it be easier to call you--

All I need is your number.

I immediately sent him both of my numbers and encouraged him to "Please call!" Within minutes the telephone rang, and the caller ID showed it was Hugh. He certainly didn't seem offended by any message I'd sent him a few days back and I was struck again by how wrong my assumptions and suppositions could be.

"Hello there," Hugh's boyish playful voice called out. "Are you always going to speak to me with poetry?"

"Oh, you mean with lyrics? I don't know. We'll have to see," I said, feeling a bit embarrassed.

"I got so nervous when I seemed to have lost your contact online. You seemed to have disappeared off of the screen for awhile." Hugh said.

"Are you ready for that swim today?"

"Yes I am. Where do we meet?" So perhaps his marking me off of his favorite list was a just a mistaken press of a button.

Hugh proceeded to give me his address. Directions weren't required since it was just down the road a few miles.

"And you can bring Trooper," Hugh added.

"Trooper is in love with you already! No one ever invites him along," I replied.

"How soon can you make it?" he asked.

"I'm practically on my way. Is there anything I can bring?"

"There's a grocery store with take out across the street if we get hungry," he replied.

Still, before I jumped into the car I took some time to reapply some sun block, leaving my back for Hugh to do. I decided to stick with eye shadow and lipstick for makeup since we were going to be swimming. Some fresh fruit was cut up for a snack. I changed into the black swimsuit that promised to make me look ten pounds lighter. Off I went, with an exuberant anticipation that waiting five weeks for a second date would foster.

The drive took only minutes. There were spacious grounds and five parking spaces surrounding the buildings at his address, which resembled a 1960s version of individual summer vacation cottages, covered in brightly painted mauve stucco, directly on the Gulf of Mexico.

He met me outdoors and motioned that it was okay to park anywhere. He was wearing khaki shorts, flip flops, but had no shirt on. He had hairy legs, arms and some of the hair on his chest was turning white. His tummy protruded a bit from above the belt line, but it looked softly round, not grossly obese. I couldn't see his eyes because he wore funky sunglasses that sported diamonds around the edges. Could those be real?

As if he read my thoughts, he commented, "These were Marilyn's sunglasses. Notice how the wrap-around sides protect the entire eye."

Marilyn had been his second wife, the one who died. He did look a bit girly in the glitzy shades, but they were perfect for protecting the eye area from the intense sun.

He showed me the guest quarters, which were smaller than my house, but adequate for a vacationer to enjoy the fabulous beach and waterfront vistas. In the center of the main room was an enormous king sized bed, which seemed to fill the room.

As we were passing through the room, he stopped and looked at it, turned and looked at me with a serious expression on his face, then moved on.

Off to the side of the room was a space where a tiny fridge, small stove, and counter were set up to act as a kitchen, or at least a modified food preparation area. The room led into a screened-in porch where an oversized futon lined the wall. It looked like a comfy spot to gaze out over the waters within the protection of the house.

The furnishings were eclectic, with lots of older antique pieces mixed in between an electric massage chair, a small round metal table and lush oriental rugs set down on top of the tile floor.

"You can leave your things here," Hugh said, pointing to a small stool stationed at the end of the bed. I dropped my beach bag there. When he left the room I changed out of my skirt and draped a scarf around my waist. I always tried to cover up the upper thighs, which I considered to be my worst feature, because they were flabby and wrinkled. I went outside with Trooper on my heels, barking and running circles around me.

"Why is he barking like that?" Hugh asked. I put out my hand in front of Trooper's nozzle to signal him to quiet down. He did not. I held up the two frisbees I had taken from the car.

"He's excited; these are his toys," I said in his defense. "Is it okay to go on the beach with the dog here?"

"Sure, it's a triple lot and the neighbors aren't even in," Hugh said.

Trooper and I ran off towards the water in delight, throwing a frisbee out into the crashing waves while Trooper raced to catch it in his mouth. The dog's exuberance was contagious and soon we were both splashing in and out of the waves, chasing after the frisbees, which got caught up in the breeze and drifted off.

Hugh seemed to have disappeared, but then he emerged from his cottage sporting swim trunks and headed towards the water. Trooper was left on the beach to play. We headed out, past the breaking point of the waves to where the water was shoulder deep. We took some time jumping the waves and letting the tide take us for a ride.

"Okay, I want to know about some of your *POF* dates," I said.

"I went on the site about a year after Marilyn died," Hugh said. "I don't respond much to the flirts and messages that someone wants to meet me. I get a good number of inquiries but most of the dates haven't progressed. I'm not looking a pen pal. So many women don't even look like their profile photos. That drives me nuts."

"Tell me about it," I said. "Why don't people take a good look in the mirror before they post information about themselves! We are not who we were in college. There shouldn't be any photos that are older than a year!"

"I don't want to associate with anyone who does drugs," Hugh said. "One woman said she didn't, but then one night she was drinking and took some over-the-counter thing and went crazy. She started biting me and must have thought it was erotic, because she was going all over my body until I had to pull her off of me and tell her to stop. I had the marks for days."

"My ex-boyfriend Scott had bitten my neck the first week we met and I sported deep red welts, which I considered to be very annoying. I like to kiss, but I'd never do that to anyone," I said.

We floated in the surf, bobbing up and down with the curves of the choppy waves.

"You know the adage, 'Live today as if it's your last'? I think that's what we should plan to do to today!" I took hold of his arm which was floating next to mine and pulled myself closer to him until we were face-to-face. I kissed him on the lips, then pulled away laughing, "There's something I want to do if this is my last day on earth. At least we can get that first kiss out of the way!"

Hugh pulled me back closer to him and proceeded to return the kiss, holding me very close to his body while the waves washed by and over us. "Whatever you do to me I'm going to do to you twice."

My legs wrapped around his hips and my body moved in unison to his as he jumped the waves. We laughed gleefully as the waters washed over us in the glittering aquamarine Gulf.

We moved together as if one in rhythm with the ocean under the cloudless sun. I hung on tightly to Hugh, buried my head in his neck and rubbed it gently in an up and down motion.

"Now you are teasing." Hugh said.

Taking his dare, I put both arms around his neck and let my body float next to his until my side and hip were brushing up against his stomach.

"This may be the only time you'll ever be able to carry me around, so take hold now!" I said.

Hugh let his arms encircle my waist, holding me close to him, while proceeding to jump the oncoming waves that were crashing over us while we laughed in delight.

"I take it back. Whatever you do to me I'm going to do three, no four, times back to you!"

My response was to slide my leg down his, slowly letting it caress the inside of his thigh, then just as slowly and deliberately slide it upwards where it lingered.

Facing together we pulled each other close. The undulating movements of his body pulsated against me, and we drifted in this seductive state until an oncoming wave swept over our heads and knocked us both over, washing us back towards shore.

Back on the beach, Trooper was frantically racing to and fro trying to locate the frisbee that one of the neighbors had thrown into the surf.

"I'd better go see if I can calm Trooper down," I said as I moved away from Hugh and waded back to shore.

Hugh followed me, and proceeded back toward his cottage, where a visitor was standing.

I began walking back when approached by another beachgoer who said, "Dogs aren't allowed on the beach. The police were called about it."

She said it in such a matter-of-fact way that I was not offended, and merely replied, "Most of this area of the beach belongs to that man there," pointing to Hugh who was standing and talking to his guest. "Thanks for playing with Trooper, though," I added before moving off.

The police never did arrive, having better things to do than pursue dog complaints on exclusive and private Longboat Key beach properties.

Dark clouds moved in and hid the horizon. Afternoon and evening storms were becoming the norm, but unfortunately didn't seem to cool the air down afterwards.

I sat snuggled on one end of the futon on the lanai of the guest cottage, content to just sit and stare out over the beach and water, watching the tropical summer storm move in.

Hugh took a chair across the room. I waited silently. Finally he got up from the chair and moved over to the futon where he sat on the other end. I scooted over towards him, and placed my legs over his. Leaning forward, I wrapped my arms around his neck, resting my head on his shoulder. I felt utterly content.

He stroked my legs gently while I stayed nestled against him, and would have been happy to remain just where I was forever.

The skies turned black. Lightning crackled cutting the sky in half with a zigzag stroke that brought back the lightness of day momentarily. "Look at that," Hugh said as the next bolt of lightning appeared instantaneously, as if a tree trunk with fiery branches was engulfing the western horizon.

"This is the most amazing lightning show I have ever witnessed!" I said.

It was if all of my prayers had been answered with one lightning bolt. Torrential rains followed the lightning, but we stayed put, content to rest in each other's arms.

The rains ended as sunset approached. We went back out to the now deserted beach and watched the sun descend below the horizon. I draped my arms around his shoulders and rested my head there.

"Thank you for this," I said.

"It's what you said you wanted—sunset on the beach," Hugh said.

"I'm expecting company tonight," I said. "My nephew is coming by with a girlfriend and plans to spend the night. I should get going."

Hugh loosened his hold and we walked back to his cottage.

I showered the sand off in the bathroom and changed into a skirt and blouse. Hugh was lounging on the massage chair when I emerged from the bathroom. I felt his eyes burning into me with a desire that made me want to touch him again. I picked up my beach bag on my way out. Trooper, who had been hiding under the table during the storm, dutifully jumped up and trotted out alongside me.

As if on cue, just hours after my company that was supposed to stay one night departed three days later, the phone rang.

It was Hugh. "What are you up to?" he asked.

"I've been waiting for you to call," I said.

"How about I come over and keep you company?"

"Your timing couldn't be more perfect," I said.

Hugh arrived by car and rang the doorbell in the garage at the back door.

He was greeted with a big hug and a long, slow kiss. From the back doorway, he could see the entire layout of the ranch style bungalow in a glance, since a wall had been removed to create an open floor plan, which made the house appear to be larger. It was a small and modest home nonetheless, no matter how many renovations were done.

Hugh was carrying a grocery store plastic bag, which contained his swimsuit and a stack of movies. I thought he'd have a more distinguished bag.

"Pick out something you'd enjoy watching," he suggested. We spread out the selection of comedies—Buster Keaton silent films, Woody Allen productions, Jack Benny reruns—and I silently perused the titles. I picked out a Woody Allen film and we went to the living room area and sat down on the couch.

"I wrote you another poem," I announced, fetching the paper with the verse written on it and handing it to him. He read silently and slowly, sometimes stopping to question a word.

How to Measure . . . a Kiss?

How do I measure your kiss?

It was deeper than the Pacific is deep.

It was higher that Mt. Everest is steep.

It was a transcendent moment I grasp to keep.

You transported me to a state of bliss!

Oh, ethereal kisses ever so sweet!

Stroke away this sadness, casting it away;

Bereft of your divine touch another day.

Summon forth more kisses without delay!

Caress this wounded soul—let us once again meet.

Kisses soft and tender take me in your embrace!

Yearning for more is all I can wish;

(&, with no other do I now want to fish;)

Starving without you in desire's anguish;

Your kiss made its endearing mark I cannot erase.

Hugh set aside the poem, leaned forward and took me into his arms, engulfing me with his. We stayed together, contented on the couch, forgetting to put a movie on.

I thought I had experienced happiness in my lifetime, but never thought I had ever achieved the state of joy and contentment that came from just holding him in my arms. I knew what it was to have time stand still, to become lost in someone's embrace, to experience the rapture of a kiss that reached deep into the soul, touching the very depths of being! Oh, that the night might never end!

In the morning I danced my way down the street, skipping on sunbeams and leaping with abandon until reaching my island friends for 7 a.m. coffee. They were all eager to hear updates on my dating escapades.

"Well," Jane demanded, once settled in with our hot coffee mugs before us.

"I think I found the one," I said.

"Which one?" asked Jane.

"It's the widower on Longboat who promises his woman diamonds. It's been six weeks since I went onto the dating website. I've had 15 dates with seven different men. The website predicted it would take about seven prospects before one settled down—*POF* even predicted he would be most likely the one!" I disclosed.

"How can you even keep all of these men straight?" laughed one of the women.

"I just jot down the current date's name on the palm of my hand!" I joked.

It wasn't so amusing when more than a couple of days went by and Hugh did not call. How could something so powerfully life changing for me not be having the same effect on him? There was nothing to do but immerse myself in rigorous physical activities that left me exhausted by the end of the day, keep busy with housework and bike rides with Trooper, and try not to be too disappointed every time I checked my messages and saw that nothing had come in from Hugh.

I wrote him a poem, but did not post it online:

> *I was thinking about you;*
>
> > *I don't know why.*
>
> *You're on my mind;*
>
> > *did we ever say goodbye?*
>
>
> *I wanted to talk to you;*
>
> > *I didn't know what to say.*
>
> *We have so much more to do together;*
>
> > *you should call without delay!*
>
>
> *All of my kisses*
>
> > *are now for you and you alone.*
>
> *Don't let this lonely heart*
>
> > *turn forever into stone.*
>
>
> *In each other's arms*
>
> > *is how nights are best spent.*

To keep you close beside me

is undoubtedly how things were meant.

When all is done, and all is said,

we could have more fun, unless you're dead!

To pass the time I went online to see what could be found out about Hugh. I no longer had any interest in going on Plenty of Fish, and systematically deleted notices that someone was interested in or wanted to meet me. If someone sent a message I would read it, but there weren't many of those, and if there were they were typically short with a comment saying the profile struck them as funny. There didn't seem to be any reason to respond.

On the web there was information about Hugh's name, various addresses and telephone number that checked out with what he had already told me. There was a list of possible relatives that matched what appeared to be his children and ex-wife.

I located the valuation on the property where his ex-wife lived. The house was valued at $350,000, not the million dollars Hugh had mentioned. However, the tax base was not always the best indicator of market value, especially if property passed between friends or relatives. It was easy to find out when he acquired the Longboat property and for what price. He bought when the market had collapsed and got a great deal.

I was surprised his second wife's name didn't appear on the list of possible relatives. A photo was located of them at a charity event, and I noticed she was absolutely gorgeous, but evidently hadn't taken Hugh's last name. On the advice of a girlfriend, I typed in just the name of the woman that appeared in the caption of the photo, on a new google search. Her obituary popped up. I clicked onto the obituary and read the paragraph that had been published in the local newspaper.

I sat in a shocked state. Hugh had never married this woman. The obituary stated that they were engaged. Why did Hugh lie about his marital status? Did he think it made him look more attractive? Did he feel like he lost the love of his life even though they hadn't taken formal vows? Did he think there was common law marriage in the State of Florida?

I couldn't believe how upset I felt by his deception. Not only had he listed being widowed as his martial status on the *POF* website, but when I asked him how long he had been widowed on our first date he had answered without clarifying the situation.

If he lied about this and exaggerated about that, what else had he been lying and exaggerating about? Could he be trusted? I would have proceeded to have a complete background check performed on Hugh if I didn't have to agree to a monthly contract that would be automatically billed to my credit card. Those "deals" were usually impossible to cancel.

I did a quick search of online court sites and was able to locate the *Sarasotaclerk.com* website from which I could conduct my own criminal background check on Hugh for free. People didn't realize that all of those background check sites were merely relying on otherwise public information. People just didn't know how to search it out on their own. Having been familiar with the transfer of most of the New York Courts' public records online, I had always been able to obtain public records from the comfort of the office. It was just as easy in Florida, once the correct websites were found.

A run of his last name pulled up his last five traffic tickets in the past eleven years: two for not wearing a seat belt; one dismissed for not having proper documentation on his person; one for an expired registration and the last for speeding in a school zone. There was nothing serious there. I felt immensely relieved, especially since I wondered whether he even had a license when he preferred taking the free trolley and bus to driving his car.

On this same website I could check out his civil litigation records as well, and found something relating to a division of property when he was divorcing his wife.

Myfloridacounty.com provided a search of all of his property records, as well as copies of his assessments and tax bills. He was clean.

I was glad I could verify his character while he would never know I did so. It was a relief that he had no criminal record. I was even happier I had figured out how to do it without subscribing to a website which required posting credit card information and committing to monthly charges.

After a few days of waiting for Hugh to call, it became too unbearable. I took matters into my own hands and dialed his number.

On the third ring, he answered. "Hello there."

"Is this my inamorato?" I asked. "If you don't know what that is, I'll have to give you another lesson."

"How are you? What are you up to?" he asked. His voice sounded friendly.

"I was just wondering the same thing about you," I said.

"I'm still in bed," he said. I looked at the clock and saw it was practically noon.

"That sounds interesting, but the day is half done!" I said.

"Maybe I'm a little depressed or turning bipolar myself. Wanna come over for a swim?" he asked. I could detect a seductive note to his voice, while I imaged him lounging lazily in the oversized bed.

I did want to go over, but when I looked out the window I saw my lawn man had just arrived. I had to talk to him before he left. "I've got to go over some instructions with my lawn guy," I replied. "What's your weekend looking like?"

"I have a party tonight and I go out with the guys on Sundays," he said.

I remembered he mentioned a weekly date with his buddies. I felt miffed that he did not invite me to the party. I didn't want our relationship to just be a private one—within a week of meeting Scott, he was introducing me to his family members and calling me his "significant other."

I wanted to say to Hugh that he wouldn't be ashamed of me, but didn't. For all I knew he could have another date lined up for Saturday and it was his nice way of telling me he was otherwise engaged.

"You sound really busy," I said while thinking how I had absolutely nothing lined up to do for the weekend.

"What about Monday and Tuesday?" he countered.

"That sounds good to me!" I answered. We hung up and I realized I had given up the chance to spend the afternoon with him. At least I could look forward to next week.

I spent the weekend watching romantic comedies on Netflix and eating popcorn with Trooper nestled up beside me on the couch.

On Monday morning I laundered the sheets and towels, swept and dusted the house and mopped the floors. I straightened the closet and started discarding stained clothing into the day's trash pickup. I contemplated what I might prepare in the way of a dinner-for-two at home. I perused recipes to see if I had all the ingredients for chicken marsala and risotto. I slowly showered, shaved, applied make up and used the blow dryer to comb out my hair until it showed signs of body. I touched up the nail polish on my toes, but decided against applying it to the fingernails. I chose a simple skirt and blouse to wear. With nothing further to do, I picked up a book, read and waited by the phone.

When the phone did not ring by 4:30 p.m. I picked it up and, with my heart noticeably palpitating and palms sweaty, I located his number in my directory. I pressed the call button. After three rings it went to voicemail. I left a brief message.

"Hi Hugh; this is Katie. Are we still on for a date tonight? Call me!" I hung up quickly, my hand visibly shaking. I was glad he was not there to see me. Then, I sat down, put on a soulful female jazz singer and did something I hadn't done in a long time: I cried.

Just a bit over an hour later the phone rang and showed that Hugh was calling back.

"Hello sweetheart," I called out on answering.

"Hello," he replied. "I didn't realize we had a date lined up for today. Wasn't it tomorrow?"

I was so glad he was calling I didn't correct him. "You were so busy over the weekend you said we'd get together this week," I said.

"I have a meeting tonight. It would have to be late. Would that be okay?"

"I'll be here," is all I said.

"I wanted to come over last night," he said.

"I was here then too," I said, wishing he had.

"Tuesday for sure," Hugh said.

"About what time?" I asked.

"I'll be back in the afternoon around 1 p.m.," he said.

"I have things to do too in the morning," I said.

"Okay, we'll see," he said.

We hung up. It wasn't until the next day, when Hugh never called back, that I realized he had forgotten about me again.

I consulted with my trusted islander advisors at morning coffee and they all said the same thing: "Don't call him; he has to make the next move. Men want to be the pursuers, and if they don't pursue you they're not worth it anyway." I listened to their advice. Even I could recognize that I wasn't important to Hugh.

I had stopped looking for other dates when I thought Hugh and I had something special going on, but it now it seemed obvious that I was not so special. He probably did have a date with another woman over the weekend. He certainly was vague. It was time to stop moping and move on.

It wasn't the first time Hugh had left me waiting by the phone, but I was determined to try to make it the last.

Nice Guy

Determined that I was not going to sit around moping and waiting for the phone to ring, (I'd done enough of that following the breakup with Scott) I went back online to review some of the inquiries I had gotten, but ignored. There were two or three that sounded interesting:

1. Scotty

    60-year-old, 5'10" nonreligious Scotsman

    Retired pilot, associates degree

    Divorced with prior longest relationship over 10 years

    Interested in feeling young again in love

    Putting his woman as his priority

    Venice

2. Braveheart

   59-year-old, 6'2", Christian – "other", divorced

   MBA still working in executive position

   Single with children over 18 not in residence with him

   Financially, mentally and physically fit

   Great sense of humor, well groomed, wine snob

   Tampa

3. Nice Guy

   65-year-old, 6', new age religion

   Adventurer, retired with bachelors degree

   Divorced with children over 18

   Loves to travel

   Passionate man who enjoys the touch of his partner

   Bradenton

I studied their profiles intently. The Scotsman was a U.S. citizen who
had also lived abroad for the better part of his life, and that was
appealing. His numerous photos of himself all were fairly good close
ups of his face; in some he wore glasses, in others not. That he made
mention of putting his woman first was suddenly very important; I
didn't want another situation where it appeared my date might be
engaging in dating with other women simultaneously. I agreed

wholeheartedly that being in love made a person feel young again.

It was Scotty's rather long *Description* of himself that was a turn off. First he warned he was sick of women who were just after his money. I would have thought retired pilots were comfortably off, but not that rich. He, like so many others, was claiming to be looking for love for the last time. A kiss, to him, was a deal breaker, and he promised to give lessons if need be. He acknowledged that everyone was getting older, and stated he wouldn't mind a woman up to 25 pounds overweight. I thought this was relative: a 4'10" woman who was 25 pounds overweight looked completely different from a 5'8" woman carrying 25 extra pounds. Still, it was refreshing to see a man who wasn't looking for perfection.

Scotty claimed that too many women were just out there for sex! That part was hard to believe. He then began a fairly detailed description of a bedroom scene in which he yearned for the "succulent lips, ecstatic moans, curves of the hips, thighs and breasts to caress" of his woman while she was spoiled by him as his grubby hands shook her. At that point I couldn't read anymore and wondered why his *Description* hadn't been censured for explicit content. I pressed the delete key to remove him from my list of matches.

Braveheart was not so explicit in his desires, and was less attractive because he lived in Tampa, which would be an hour and one-half drive away. Braveheart, following an alleged nasty divorce, was not afraid to love again, and claimed to be loyal, clean living and looking for his partner, best friend, confidant and lover. His idea of a first date was boring, and when he stated that, "unlike most guys I would like to meet over a cup of coffee to determine if there is chemistry," little did he know that over 90% of the men had the same idea. Having a cup of coffee was a cheap way to conduct a first date, while determining if a second date would be following. I couldn't understand how he could claim to be a Christian, and also claim to be "other." The fact that he was still working also meant we would only have weekends together, given the distance between us. A three-hour round trip drive just to get together for a date consisting of a cup of coffee was not appealing, and he was eliminated on that basis alone.

I reread Nice Guy's *Profile*. He was getting extra points for brevity. There was less to find fault with when less information was provided. I didn't know what the New Age religion was, but figured it meant he didn't go to church. It was a real plus that he lived in nearby Bradenton, but then I remembered that Bradenton covered a lot of territory, and could also become a one-hour drive, just to meet. Since he had messaged me expressing an interest in meeting I decided to just go for it. I had nothing to lose but the upsetting memories of waiting around for Hugh. I wanted to put that in the past as quickly as possible. I wrote to him:

Hello Mr. Nice Guy,

Sorry for the delay in getting back to you. I enjoyed reading your Profile. I, too, like to travel whenever I can manage to get away. Are you still interested in meeting?

Regards,

Katie

I wasn't too concerned about writing long emails back and forth anymore. The men had my *Profile* to review, and I was fairly explicit about my interests. I couldn't remember if Nice Guy had messaged me before or after my revisions, especially the one detailing a *First Date*, but didn't really care. It was a spoof after all and anyone I went out with would understand that.

I felt immensely relieved that I had taken steps to move on and away from Hugh, and gratified when I soon received a reply from Nice Guy.

Hi Katie,

What a funny First Date you have planned. I'm ready for it! What are you doing this weekend?

Regards,

Edward

Without delay I messaged back.

Hi Edward,

I hope I'll be meeting you this weekend! How about Saturday we plan a general meet to explore the island? It can get a bit crowded, but is worth the drive.

What do you think?

Katie

It wasn't long before I received his answer.

Katie,

I could plan to meet with you around 2 p.m. if you'd like to suggest a place.

Edward

I immediately responded:

Let's meet at the City Pier and we can take it from there. Maybe we can start with a picnic on the beach. Do you need directions?

He messaged back:

Sounds good. No, I know the way. See you Saturday.

I felt immensely pleased with the progress I was making, and relieved that I would have someone with whom to spend the weekend. There was nothing worse than having nothing special lined up to do for an entire weekend.

Saturday proved to be the hottest day of the summer thus far. I showered after working out in the gym, but by the time I walked the ten minutes it took to get to the pier I was soaked with perspiration. I didn't want to smell like Benjamin did when we first met.

Edward had called when he had gotten to the pier ahead of me and let me know he was wearing navy blue shorts and a white button down shirt. We were still talking on our cell phones when I spotted him at the end of the pier. I closed the cover of the cell phone. At least there was a bit of a mildly cooling breeze at the end of the pier.

"Hi Edward, so nice to meet you," I announced as I approached him.

Edward took a step forward to meet me, and stopped in front of me. "Yes, how are you?" he asked as if we hadn't just been talking on the phone. We stood facing each other.

"It's better here than on the beach. That's the trouble with these afternoon dates; you can really call them hot dates and you have to learn how to beat the heat," I said as I pulled out two ice cold sodas from my beach bag. I held up one diet coke and one ginger ale. "Which do you prefer?" I asked. The drinks were all I thought to throw into the beach bag as I was exiting the house. I recalled mentioning suggesting a picnic on the beach, but had packed nothing more. We could always buy a sandwich and take it with us.

Edward reached out and took the ginger ale from my hand. "Thank you very much," he said as he cracked open the lid and began drinking it. I could see the sweat glistening on his brow. We sat down on a fisherman's bench overlooking the Bay.

"How was the drive?" I asked.

"It took me over an hour to get here," he responded. "The island traffic was the worst part."

He must live quite a bit inland if it had taken so long. I gave him a quick examination as he was speaking. He was a relatively young looking 65-year-old even though his thick hair had turned completely white. He really was 6' tall. He was very slender but for a small tummy, and had a clean cut look. Very few men in their 60s were completely lean, unless they worked at it everyday. His clothes looked pristine and he got extra points for that. He reminded me of someone who knew how to get along quietly in life. His username suit him perfectly. He looked like a nice guy, safe and dependable.

"Tell me what you did in your pre-retirement years," I asked.

"For half my career I taught social studies in a Catholic school. When my marriage broke up I decided I wanted to move, so relocated here and got a job in the local Board of Education. I taught ninth graders for over 15 years, and I was glad to take an early retirement when my pension plan was fully vested. I don't miss it," Edward said.

"I practiced law in New York, and I don't miss it either," I said. "As long as I can make do on my income from investments I'm content, although I am wavering on whether to renew my registration at the end of the year." I wondered how much retirement income he could be deriving from teaching. It was surprising he had listed his religion as New Age when he was obviously Catholic. It was hard to be a Catholic nowadays amid all the scandals of the church.

As if reading my mind, Edward said, "I am celebrating because I now get three checks every month: one from the Catholic school, one from the public, and social security." He made no comment about my profession.

"That's sounds comfortable. Many of the Catholic schools in New York never offered a retirement plan for their teachers." I remembered how disgusted I was when I learned how little those teachers earned compared to their public school counterparts. It was not a decent living wage, but something a two-wage-earner couple would do to scrape by.

"We had a very good package," he said.

"Tell me, was it challenging to teach?" I asked.

"Actually, I could do it in my sleep," he replied. "The challenge was keeping the kids in line. I don't miss having to deal with teenagers everyday," he said. "I enjoy my calm and quiet."

He looked like someone who was used to some measure of solitude. It troubled me a bit that he would have characterized his career as dull.

"I enjoyed the photos you posted of your travels to Tahiti, New Zealand and Alaska. Alaska—now there's somewhere I would like to be today!" I commented.

"I enjoy planning trips. I can afford to travel about twice a year."

"Do you travel alone or go with groups?"

"I usually use one tour company and book most everything through it, including side trips. It's easier to let someone else handle the details and arrange for things like transportation in places where I've never been and don't know," he said.

"That's true," I said, "although when my kids and I traveled to Europe last year we planned the entire trip on our own, based on places we wanted to see. My daughter had enough points on her credit cards to cover our lodging when we weren't staying with friends. I was able to easily book air and rail travel via the internet. We couldn't have afforded a trip to major European capitals otherwise," I said. "Why don't we take the trolley and travel the scenic coastline? It's air conditioned!"

"That sounds good to me," Edward replied. We strolled down the crowded pier, but picked up the pace as the trolley was spotted approaching its stop. We entered to find it relatively crowded, but we could still find a bench seat that seated two. I took the window seat, which was wide enough so that when we sat our bodies were not touching. The ride was slow but coolly agreeable. There was not much to point out along the way; peeks of the water along the scenic highway were about the most interesting thing to see.

"How many children do you have?" I asked.

"I just have one daughter," Edward replied. "She is mentally challenged and my wife and I spent the better part of our marriage worrying about her, finding special needs programs and having her trained to become functional and self-sufficient. Those concerns put a real strain on our marriage, and probably was the main cause of our breakup. My daughter now holds a job and has her own place, not too far from me."

"I sorry to hear it took such a toll on you," I said. "I know what it is to worry about a child, but not exactly in the same way you did. Troubles with our children were something that actually held my husband and me together."

Edward did not ask for further details, so I offered none.

As the trolley approached the Bridge Street exit of Bradenton Beach I asked, "Would you like to get off here and walk around?"

"Sure," Edward replied.

We alighted and strolled along the quiet and fairly pedestrian-free main street. We walked out as far as we could on the pier and took a seat on a bench. We were refreshed by the most delightful cross breeze over the intercoastal waterway.

"I think we found the best spot of the day!" I said. We were content to sit and remain cool under the heat of the afternoon sun. I silently vowed this would be the absolute last date I would book in the afternoon hours. I was thirsty again and was feeling a bit hungry. I couldn't remember if I had even had lunch. We chatted comfortably, mostly about Edward's planned travels, and I about my upcoming trip up north. It was easy and casually entertaining.

"It's going to be an effort, but why don't we move on?" I asked.

"Okay," Edward said. He was utterly agreeable.

We walked back towards the trolley stop and spotted one approaching. I waved my arms frantically as I sprinted across the street, Edward just behind me. We made it to the spot where we had exited the previous trolley, but this one would not stop for us. I stood in complete bewilderment.

"Isn't this the spot?" I asked as I moved in an agitated manner to check the posted sign. "This is really annoying. It's going to be another 20 – 30 minutes before another trolley comes!"

Edward said nothing but did not look too upset. We walked a very short distance to where the official trolley stop was.

"I can't believe it wouldn't stop and wait when we were so close," I said as I paced at the trolley stop angrily, which although uncovered was at least under the shade of a palm tree. The cooling breeze was nonexistent there and I looked longingly out over the Gulf water. I was wearing my swimsuit and was ready for a swim. If Edward was similarly outfitted we could have gone in.

"Did you bring a swimsuit?" I asked.

"Yes, but I left it in the car," he said. It wouldn't do him any good there. It reminded me of Flipshot who really wasn't ready for a date on the beach even though he knew that was the plan. It would have been so much more fun to jump in the water and cool down. It certainly would have provided some relief from the scorching afternoon sun. I tried not to show my annoyance and was glad some women tourists joined us and began making small talk about the trolley schedule and stops. We were comfortable enough being in each other's presence but not having to talk all of the time. I did wish we were going on the beach though, which beckoned with its breaking waves and was merely a few steps west.

"Are you hungry?" I asked, knowing I was, and remembering the picnic that was supposed to be a part of the date.

"I suppose," he replied. His tall lean build evidenced that eating was not all that important to him.

The trolley arrived, nearly 45 minutes after the other one had passed us by. The remainder of the ride to Coquina took less than ten minutes and I realized that if it hadn't been so damn hot we could have walked there, along the beach, in under twenty minutes, which would have been much better than waiting impatiently for the trolley. It struck me how most of the men, but for Sarasota Bill and Diamonds4u/Hugh, were more than content for me to plan the entire date.

On arrival we made our way over to the concession stand which was in the process of closing for the day.

"Isn't there anything we can still get?" I asked the woman in the process of closing up. I felt ravenous.

"You can get something from the cooler or prepackaged," she said

I looked at Edward. "Are you interested in anything here?" I asked, to which he shrugged his shoulders.

"Will you get me a scoop of butter pecan ice cream," I ordered. The clerk dutifully took a small cup and proceeded to fill it with one scoopful, which made me wish I had ordered the larger size. In the few seconds it took for it to be handed over the counter, much of the ice cream was melting into a pool around in the bottom of the cup.

"That'll be $3.99," the woman said. I fished into my beach bag and gathered four dollar bills. I noticed that Edward had stepped back and away from the counter, much like Eliot had done at our dinner out. I tried not to hold it against him that he was not springing for the treat, and tried to recall if in one of the revisions I had changed my *First Date* from a "going Dutch" experience. I thought I had, and knew I had made one of my *interests* "being wined and dined."

No matter what I had said or written I still expected the man to at least offer to pay. Maybe times had really changed in the 35 years since I was on the dating scene. Little did Edward know that little omission changed my opinion of him. It may not have been fair, but that was the way it was. I just wasn't going to be too interested in any man who was cheap. A good woman was someone on whom any man should be willing to spend his money!

That cheapness was what formed my generally unfavorable opinion not only of Edward, but also of Eliot, Benjamin, and in part with Surfman and Tony. They were five of the eight men I had met online and perhaps were representative of the majority of single available men on the dating scene. Maybe their frugality was in part what was keeping them single. I recalled Surfman had paid for a glass of wine before he offered me a homemade meal of rice and beans, and Tony just directed me to leave the tip following our meal. All of the men had purported to be financially secure, and most hinted at greater wealth, yet some didn't want to spend any money.

Scott had always taken me out to dine, and I felt I had reciprocated by cooking and serving him meals at home. The difference it made when a man spent a couple of dollars was really amazing. It really took so little to come across as a generous, kind and giving man! Going into the last third of an average lifetime should have served as a reminder to men that one's wealth had no value in the grave. What were they saving their money for after all? I was not inclined to try to teach old dogs new tricks. If they didn't know how to show a woman they appreciated and cherished her that was their problem. Maybe there were other women on the dating scene who didn't care who picked up the tab.

Money had never been an object between my husband and me. Whatever I wanted I got, but I never felt I asked for anything too wild or extravagant. My husband would have bought me lots of jewels during our travels and holidays together, and it was I who usually opted for more practical gifts. He usually spent far more on me than I would have asked. I just expected that this behavior was the norm, not the exception to the rule. I was finding out otherwise.

Edward and I sat on the elevated deck on the Gulf's expansive white beach while I savored the last spoonful of the ice cream.

"Look, here comes the northbound trolley," I called out while standing up in anticipation of making it to the trolley stop. Edward followed my lead. There had been no need for the sprint to the trolley since once we alighted we sat for fifteen minutes while the driver took his break. He did us the courtesy of leaving the air conditioning running during the stop. The ride back was uneventful and I spent most of the time looking out of the window.

"Trooper usually gets his dinner around 5 p.m.," I told Edward, "so I'll probably head back to the house once we get to the pier." I did not invite him over.

"It's been a good afternoon," Edward said.

"Talk about a really hot date!" I said. "I'm sorry we didn't jump into the Gulf when we were at Coquina."

The trolley pulled into the parking lot.

"Would you like to get together again?" Edward asked.

"Maybe," I said.

"Look, why don't we leave it that if you'd like another date you just call me, okay?" Edward said.

"That sounds perfect," I said. I began to walk away, but turned to give another wave goodbye. He was already heading up the street with his back to me. Edward really was a nice guy. I appreciated his candor and how clearly things were set forth concerning any future dates. He was a good conversationalist and had been interesting. I didn't understand why overall I found him dull. I could blame it on Hugh. He did not excite me, yet he epitomized someone who would be honest, reliable and dependable; someone who shared my core values even if he rejected organized religion.

Why was I still drawn to another man who was obviously not enamored of me and had treated me disrespectfully? In the following days when I sat home alone, I pondered this question, wondering if there was some quirk in human nature that made seemingly unavailable persons more enticing.

Not Quite Caught

When I thought over the events of the past seven weeks I came to the following conclusions:

--Thanks to the internet, there was an active dating scene for seniors (as well as anyone else of any age who wanted to date) of which I had been formerly unaware.

--There seemed to be adequate screening methods so there was less fear and apprehension over meeting a relative stranger. I believed I could tell a lot about a man by how he wrote and spoke. Meetings in public places provided for a safety net. Of course, a lot of information that was provided by each user had to be taken on faith. Background checks were easy to do online.

I was still upset by how many silly lies I had caught men in, and how those little lies ended up affecting my desire to pursue a relationship with them. Men did not have to lie about their age! Getting caught in a lie was always going to be far worse than just telling the truth. Everyone was starting out with a blank slate.

--No one had to sit at home alone unless by choice, since *POF* allowed for all different types of choices: women seeking women for friendship and companionship; women seeking men for friendship, *etc.*

--The dating experience had felt a bit like being back in high school, but overall that was a good thing. It was a thrill to feel the rush and uncertainties of youth again!

--I had actually been a bit overwhelmed by all the choices. I had gone from having no one interested in me to having so many that I may not have been giving each man a fair trial. A bad first impression was fatal to the possibility of future dates. Clean clothes were a must! There was a good likelihood that if I had met almost any one of the men I'd gone out with prior to signing on *POF* I would have been more likely to want to go out on more dates with him. The plethora of possibilities made it easy to find fault with a date and move onto another.

--When thinking about the eight men I had met, I was happy that one asked me to marry him, and three left open the possibility of future dates with me. Two just didn't seem to be a good personality match— one did not seem ready for a relationship and with the other, the proverbial "chemistry" just wasn't right. My two personal favorites unfortunately did not seem to be as taken with me as I was with them. I could understand Bill's reticence to move forward. Hugh remained a big disappointment, yet I recognized I couldn't have said or done anything differently to make him like me more. I wished there were some magic formula in affairs of the heart and I could have made him like me as much as I liked him.

--Men wanted shapely women. Most of them would come right out and say that they would not be attracted to overweight women. Scott always had, I remembered. After my online dating experience, our relationship seemed much more special. I wrote "All men want shapely women," on a note card and posted it prominently on the refrigerator door.

I clicked onto my *Profile* and deleted most of my *description*. The *Intent* was changed to "wanting to marry." I deleted both of the photos. I went to *First Date*, and deleted the entire post. Without photos and description, and with intent to get married, it was most unlikely anyone would contact me, which was okay by me for now because I was ready to take a break from actively seeking new dates.

It had been fun, but it had taken most of my time and energy, to correspond with prospects, arrange for meetings, and then attend the dates, some of which had only been an hour or so, but others entire days. I could be content with just having my summer travel plans to look forward to, and have time to finish some books on my summer reading list. As much as I would enjoy having a man around to share my life with, I did not have to work on it incessantly. I was getting older, but then so was everyone else.

It felt good just to have met some men around my own age who were still interested in dating me. I noticed a certain camaraderie with men of similar age that was easygoing and fun. I also noted a certain discomfort if the age difference was more than ten or so years, which could be overcome if both people were mutually attractive to each other.

No matter what the ages, I liked best the men who had challenged themselves in their careers and had pursued higher education. They appealed to me perhaps because I had worked my way through college and law school, and chosen a very challenging profession which had kept me intellectually stimulated almost every day. Someone who had just managed to get by in life, who hadn't tried to set and accomplish more difficult goals, I found to be rather uninspired and insipid.

We may be getting older, but we weren't dead yet!

Just as I was contemplating which, if any, of the men I had met I might yet follow up with, the telephone rang.

Made in the USA
Charleston, SC
20 November 2014